D1172675

VIKKI VANISHES

Also by Peni R. Griffin:

Otto from Otherwhere
A Dig in Time
Hobkin
The Treasure Bird
Switching Well
The Brick House Burglars
The Maze

(Margaret K. McElderry Books)

VIKKI VANISHES

PENI R. GRIFFIN

Margaret K. McElderry Books

Margaret K. McElderry Books
An imprint of Simon & Schuster Children's Publishing Division
1230 Avenue of the Americas
New York, New York 10020

The text of this book is set in 10/14 Bookman.

Printed in the United States of America
Printed on recycled paper
First edition
10   9   8   7   6   5   4   3   2   1

Library of Congress Cataloging-in-Publication Data

Griffin, Peni R.
    Vikki vanishes / Peni R. Griffin.—1st ed.
        p. cm.
    Summary: Her habit of lying to her mother and older sister
Vikki makes it hard for Nikki to convince people that Vikki's recently
returned father is responsible for her disappearance.
    ISBN 0-689-80028-2
    [1. Sisters—Fiction. 2. Child abuse—Fiction. 3. Kidnapping,
parental—Fiction. 4. Fathers and daughters—Fiction.] I. Title.
PZ7.G88136Vi   1995
[Fic]—dc20   94-48340
                                                                   CIP
                                                                    AC

For Kerry, for obvious reasons

Contents

VIKKI VANISHES

ONE

Nikki Goes through the Roof

NIKKI HAD BEEN SENT TO HER ROOM—AGAIN. SHE climbed onto the bed and bounced, chanting, "It's no fair! I don't care! It's no fair! I don't care!"

Her big sister, Vikki, rapped on the door. "If you don't stop jumping on the bed, you won't get any ice cream for supper."

Nikki stood still and stuck her tongue out at the door. "I'm not jumping on the bed!"

"Right," said Vikki. "You sit there and think about Mrs. Lozano's poor flowers till Mom comes home."

Nikki plunked down onto the pillows and glared at the door as Vikki's footsteps moved away. She hadn't meant to hurt Mrs. Lozano's flowers; and she'd told a perfectly good story, afterward, about a stray dog doing the damage before she could run him off. Of course when Rudy from down the street said he'd seen her chase a ball into the flower bed, everybody'd believed him instead of her. It wasn't fair! She hadn't thrown the ball there on purpose; and she'd only told the lie because she was so tired of getting blamed for things.

Nikki felt as if she'd spent the whole summer in this room she shared with Vikki, and here it was only July. She was sick of the sight of it. Even with both windows open and the fan on, it was too hot; and she was tired of her stuffed animals, puzzles, and books. She'd already been spanked once this week for going through Vikki's things, and they weren't interesting enough to do it again. All she wanted right now was out!

Suddenly she remembered the mouse men.

The landlady had sent the mouse men with traps and poison, and they had gone into the attic through the ceiling of the closet right here in this room! Old Baldy in the other half of the duplex had complained because he didn't want his cat catching poisoned mice. Nikki had complained because they wouldn't let her go into the attic with them. She'd never been in an attic. Mom said this one was unfinished and would be boring, but she hadn't been up there, either, so what did she know? With no one around to stop her, and the whole afternoon to work with, Nikki ought to be able to look around up there and get back before Vikki even knew she was gone.

Nikki leaped off the bed, grabbed Vikki's desk chair, and dragged it to the closet. It was a pretty big closet, Vikki's clothes hanging on one side of the door and Nikki's on the other, with room in between. Nikki had only to kick a few shoes out of the way to fit the chair in. The chair didn't raise her high enough, though.

2

Nikki dragged Vikki's suitcase off the shelf above Vikki's clothes, and balanced it across the chair. Better, though wobbly and still not tall enough. Nikki rummaged through the toy box till she found the baton from her Halloween drum-majorette costume. With this, she poked the board covering the hole in the ceiling until it no longer lay straight across the opening. Then she shoved it aside. This made a certain amount of noise, but Nikki could hear Vikki playing the radio in the kitchen. She'd be okay.

It took Nikki three tries, using the wall, the shelf, and all the strength of her body, to get up through the hole. At last, though, she hauled herself into the attic.

Oof, it was hot! Stripes of light through the circular blades of the attic fan lay on the foamy pink insulation, and more light came through the dormer window sticking out the front of the roof. Balancing on her bare feet on the nearest beam, Nikki crossed to the window.

The street and yard were silent and seemed far away. Old Baldy backed his Jeep out of the driveway. Rudy skimmed by on his skateboard, zipping around Old Baldy's bumper. Mrs. Lozano knelt in her flower bed, trying to repair the damage. The ball must've done some of that, Nikki assured herself. Her feet weren't big enough to squash that many flowers.

Nikki turned away as Old Baldy drove off. It was neat to be here, no one knowing where she was, but so hot she could hardly breathe. Taking a long step to another beam, Nikki wondered whether Old Baldy's closet also had a hole in its ceiling.

Nikki went exploring, avoiding a mousetrap that looked like a dish of glue. Sure enough, in a line with the square opening she'd come up through, another board was laid across another pair of beams. From here she could move it easily. Below was a dim space, floored by shoes. A wedge of light lay across them, showing that the closet door was partly open.

Ever since Old Baldy had moved in, Nikki had wondered what his half of the duplex was like. Vikki told her not to be so nosy, but couldn't explain the strange noises he made, or the odd hours he kept. If he turned out to be a Mafia bad guy, and Nikki turned him in to the FBI and got a million-dollar reward, that would show Vikki—and everybody else, too! She lowered herself into the hole and dropped past Old Baldy's clothes—shirts on one side, pants on the other.

Landing, Nikki slipped on the shoes, and fell *plunk* on her behind. Scrambling to her feet, she opened the closet door fully. This room was shaped just like hers and Vikki's, only backward, and much emptier. The bed was untidily made, and the dresser piled with stuff—books, Dr Pepper cans, stray socks, and a pair of handcuffs! Thrilled, Nikki picked them up from between somebody's baby picture and a book with a starship on the cover. They wouldn't open, but her hand slipped easily in and out of their rings.

Cops used handcuffs, Nikki knew from TV; but bad guys had them, too, sometimes. Old Baldy wasn't a cop. He'd wear a uniform if he were. She put the handcuffs back where she'd found them, and went to explore the rest of the house.

Nikki had often thought that, if she were a crook, she'd hide her good stuff in the kitchen and the bathroom, because TV cops never searched in those places. Old Baldy's bathroom was disappointingly ordinary. In his kitchen he had a whole drawerful of gum, and a pantry full of cat food and chili. Nowhere were there any diamonds, bundles of money, or bloody weapons. Nikki couldn't even find the cat, though she'd heard it over here all morning—"meow, meow, meow," loud and long. Beginning to lose hope of her FBI reward, Nikki went on to the living room.

All idea of rewards went straight out of her head. Old Baldy had the biggest TV she'd ever seen, and one whole bookcase full of videotapes! Monster movies, comedies, and science fiction shows rose higher than her head. She couldn't watch all this stuff in a week!

Nikki thought fast. Till Old Baldy came home, there'd be no one to stop her watching whatever she wanted. The blinds were down, so no one could see her from outside, and Vikki wouldn't come looking for her till dinner. If she kept the sound down real low, there'd be nothing to give her away. If only she could figure out how to use the VCR!

She couldn't, though. When Nikki had watched tapes at her friends' houses, she'd never been allowed to work the machine, and Mom always said they couldn't afford to get their own. She could get this one to say that it was playing, but she couldn't figure out how to turn the TV on. No amount of button pushing or pulling had the least effect.

Disgusted, Nikki growled at the TV and put back the tape she'd picked out. This place was turning out to be a bust. The living room had no good hiding places for Mafia evidence, and the apartment had only one room left. Maybe that would hold the payoff, though. She couldn't imagine what Old Baldy needed a second bedroom for, and the noises from his house were loudest in Mom's bedroom, which shared a wall with this last room. Plus, she noticed as she returned to the hall, the door was closed. All the other doors, even some of the cupboards, had been open. Why was this room different? Nikki turned the knob.

The first thing she saw was a model-railroad layout on a table taking up most of the room. The second thing was a gun case—definite bad-guy evidence, with its huge padlock, rifles, pistols, and big black guns she didn't know the names of. There'd be lots of time to tell the feds about that, though. First she wanted to check out the train.

It wasn't just a model-train set. It was a whole little world laid out on a table. Two trains, one for freight and one for passengers, could go around on two sets of tracks, through a tunnel under a mountain, over a bridge, through fields and hills and a town. The town had stores, houses, people—even dogs and cats. Tiny goats drank below a plastic waterfall that tumbled down the mountain, turned into a river, and finally filled a lake where ducks and canoes paddled. Horses and cows grazed around the farms, and little people went about their business all over the tabletop.

Nikki had to walk all the way around it to see everything, and on the way she found the controls, hidden underneath the mountain. When she pushed the "on" switch, she recognized the sound at once; this was the source of all those strange noises! The trains rumbled around the tracks, whistling at the curves. She could make them speed up, slow down, switch tracks—this was the coolest thing she'd ever seen! Not that it couldn't be better. If that road there had moving cars on it, and you fixed it so the arms of the railroad-crossing sign came down and the cars stopped to let the train go by...if you put sailboats on the lake...if there were a forest, with bears and mountain lions—

"Hello," said Old Baldy. "What you doing?"

Nikki hadn't heard him coming over the noise of the train! What now? With a slap she turned off the controls. "I'm sorry!"

"I should hope so. How'd you get in?"

Nikki found she had a lie all ready to go. "I was trying to help your cat," she said. "You know where the mouse men got into the attic that time, at the tops of the closets? I heard her crying up there, so I climbed up, and she was caught in a pan of glue. So I got her loose. She scratched me, see?" She held out the arm she had scratched on Mrs. Lozano's rosebush.

Old Baldy frowned sympathetically. "Got you pretty good."

"Uh-huh." Nikki relaxed inside. "And then she jumped down through your closet."

"Why'd you follow her?"

"I was afraid the glue stuff was poison, so I wanted to catch her and wash it off."

"That was nice of you, after she'd scratched you so bad."

"I didn't want her to die. But by the time I got down here she was hiding. And I came in here looking, and saw the train, and I wanted to see how it works. It's a really cool train!"

7

"Yeah, it is," said Old Baldy. "You're a really cool liar, too. If I hadn't just gotten back from dropping Fuzzface off at the vet's, I might even believe you." He held out his hand. "Come on. Who's home at your place? Your sister? Let's go talk to Vikki."

Nikki put her hands behind her back. "No."

"No? You got a better suggestion?"

Nikki made a dash for it but Old Baldy was nearly as wide as the door, and caught her with one quick motion. Up into the air she went, kicking and struggling, as his hands closed around her ankles and he dangled her upside down like a fish. "Hold still," he said, "or I might drop you by accident."

Nikki stopped fighting, suddenly aware of the hard wood floor a few inches from her head. Old Baldy carried her through the kitchen, out to the back porch the two apartments shared, and home—where Nikki knew she would spend the rest of the summer locked in her room.

TWO

Vikki Nearly Dies of Embarrassment

THE PUBLIC RADIO STATION WAS FINISHING AN AFTER-noon of jazz, and the biscuits were ready for the oven, when Mr. Grant from the other half of the duplex appeared at the screen door. Nikki was dangling upside down from his hands. "Knock, knock," he said.

What the—? Vikki ran to open the door. "Nikki! What've you been doing?"

"Nothing," said Nikki, red-faced. "Make him put me down!"

Mr. Grant stepped inside with his captive. "Put your hands on the floor, and I'll ease you over," he said. "If I just set you down you'll hurt yourself."

Nikki obeyed, and Mr. Grant lowered her feet till she could stand. She at once straightened and pointed at him. "He's in the Mafia," she announced. "He's got a bunch of guns, and handcuffs, and—and secret video-tapes, and—"

"Stop it, Nikki, or I'll wash your mouth out with soap!" Vikki wanted to sink through the floor. Here she was, all covered with sweat and flour. Nikki was telling lies and doing heaven knew what, a neighbor was in the house—though he didn't seem too angry—and Mom was due home any minute! At least things couldn't get worse. "How'd you get out of the room?" she demanded.

Nikki folded her arms and glared. "See if I give you any of my reward money when the feds come and get him!"

"How do you know I'm Mafia and not a fed?" asked Mr. Grant, pulling out his wallet. "Or a cop, or a P.I., which is what I am? See—there's my license." He squatted to Nikki's level and showed her a card. "Lots of people have guns besides bad guys."

Nikki glared at the wallet. "What's a P.I.?"

"A private investigator," said Vikki, inwardly thrilled. If only he weren't so bald and middle-aged! "He investigates crimes for people, but he's not the police. You know, like Nancy Drew. Tell him you're sorry for saying such horrible things about him."

"How was I supposed to know?" Nikki scowled. "Make him say he's sorry for carrying me upside down!"

Vikki sighed, and put the biscuits in the oven. "I'm sorry about Nikki, Mr. Grant. What's she done this time? And how did she do it? She's supposed to be shut in her room."

"I found her playing with my model railroad," said Mr. Grant, replacing his wallet and taking out a packet of Juicy Fruit. "She says she got in through the attic access in the back-bedroom closets, and I expect it's true. I've got the doors and windows pretty well sealed up." He offered the gum to Nikki, who made a face at him. Vikki slapped her bottom lightly and accepted when he offered her a stick. "I never even thought about the attic access. Guess I'll have to now." He unwrapped a stick of gum for himself.

"I didn't make a mess at all!" protested Nikki.

"That's probably true, too," said Mr. Grant. "She didn't hurt anything that I noticed. I wouldn't be too hard on her. Being carried upside down by a suspected Mafioso must be bad enough punishment for most things, and she won't do it again—will you, kid?"

"Not in a million jillion trillion years," said Nikki, looking hopeful.

"You did tell me a lie, though," said Mr. Grant. "Trying to make me think you were doing me a favor by trying to help my cat!"

Nikki looked away, with her stubbornest expression on her face.

Vikki wanted to slap her, but didn't. Mom would do that when she got home. "Thanks for being so nice about it," she said. "I'm afraid Nikki's a bit of a handful, but we'll see she doesn't bother you again."

"Yeah, well, we're all handfuls when we're that tall."

Vikki heard a car in the driveway and grabbed Nikki's hand. "Last chance to say you're sorry before Mom gets home."

Nikki sighed and looked too far up, so her eyes must have been focused on his bald head instead of his face. "I'm sorry I got in your house and played with your train without asking and lied to you, Mr. Grant, and I hope your cat gets better real soon." Her eyes shifted down-

11

ward and she frowned interestedly. "What's wrong with her, anyway?"

"She broke her tail," Mr. Grant said, stepping toward the door. "I think she must have caught it in something. She hid under the couch and howled till I finally remembered I had some chicken liver I could lure her out with."

"Poor little thing," said Vikki. "I hope she's better soon."

Mom was climbing the back porch steps as Mr. Grant stepped outside. She looked the way she always did at the end of the day—rumpled and frowning. After being a receptionist in a busy office all day, she said, sometimes, that she was all smiled out. All the same she summoned up a smile from somewhere, with visible effort, when she saw Mr. Grant. He held the door open for her.

"Hi, y'all," said Mom. "What's going on?"

"His cat broke her tail," said Nikki. Vikki, still holding on to her, could feel how tense and hopeful she was, as if there were a chance everybody would start talking about the cat and forget to punish her.

As soon as Mr. Grant crossed the porch to his place, Mom's smile collapsed and she asked, "Okay, what was it? Did Nikki hurt his cat?"

"No!" yelped Nikki.

"No," said Vikki. "Nikki, tell her about the closet."

Every detail had to be dragged out of Nikki one at a time. Mom looked more and more tired as the story progressed, till she finally laid her head down on the table and said, "Nikki, why are you so bad all the time? Why can't you just mind your sister and be good?"

"I don't know how," said Nikki.

Vikki bit her tongue to keep from saying anything, and buttered biscuits.

12

Mom made a disgusted sound. "You don't try! I was feeling good tonight, too. That cute guy in the mail room finally asked me out. We're going dancing Saturday night, Vikki—I hope you didn't have a date."

"No," said Vikki, trying to sound pleased. "That's great, Mom." She didn't know why Mom was always so anxious to go out with men. Not one of the boyfriends she'd had since Nikki's father moved out had ever lived up to her expectations.

"And now I have to come home and spank my little girl," Mom went on, "and I don't want to."

"Don't do it then," said Nikki. "Nobody's making you. I'm too big to be spanked, anyway."

"You don't get off that easy," said Mom. "Get the hairbrush."

"Couldn't it wait till after supper?" suggested Vikki, looking at the steam rising from the hot dinner. Spanking Nikki was a long job; everything would be half cold before it was done. And it wasn't as if it ever accomplished anything.

"I want to get it over with." Mom sighed. "March, Nikki."

Of course Nikki claimed not to be able to find the brush. Vikki found it in the clothes hamper, where it couldn't possibly have gotten by itself, but she said nothing about that. Nikki didn't need any more punishments. Vikki stood in the hall pretending to look at an Avon catalog while the spanking went on.

The doorbell rang.

Vikki groaned, tried to dust some of the flour off her shorts, and went to the door, praying it wasn't another neighbor with another complaint. She didn't think the man she saw on the porch lived around here, though. He

13

smiled at her, displaying a set of teeth stained brown. "Uh...Hi, Vikki."

He was an ordinary-looking guy in jeans and work shirt, certainly none of the teachers from her high school. Possibly he was someone she was supposed to know from Mom's work. "Hi," Vikki said. "What can I do for you?"

"Uh...You don't remember me, do you?" He moved his head. "No, of course not. You haven't seen me since you were six."

Six? What had happened when she was—? Oh. But that idea was crazy. He couldn't be—

"I'm Dave," said the man. "Your—uh—Dave Baum. Your daddy."

Inside, Nikki howled furiously.

Vikki stared at the man on the porch. "My...daddy? But—"

"Yeah, I know," he said, getting his wallet out of his back pocket. "But don't be mad at me. I was looking through the papers awhile back, and I saw this." He pulled a raggedy piece of newspaper out of the bill slot— the write-up, including her picture, from the high school orchestra competition at the end of the school year. "And I said to myself, That's my girl!" He wasn't smiling anymore. "And I thought about what a rat I'd been, running out on you and Monica, and...Well, I got a job now, and I'm starting over, and I really wanted to come by and— and meet you." He looked at the newspaper. "It's a real cute picture, but in real life you're—you wouldn't think an old boy like me could make something as pretty as you, would you?"

Pretty? Her, now? Vikki wiped sweat off her nose, heart

rapping away at top speed. Her mouth was dry and fumbly.

"Don't you have anything to say to your dad?" he asked wistfully. "Hello, good-bye, get out of my life?"

Vikki's conscience kicked her. This was her *father*, for crying out loud. She should do something, not stand here staring at him, no matter how confusing this sudden reappearance was, no matter how little she knew about him or how little she understood what she felt herself. Either welcome him, or close the door in his face—and she didn't want to close the door in his face. "Of course I'm glad to see you!" she said, the statement becoming true all at once as she spoke.

"I don't mean to come barging in on your life," said...Dad. "I wanted to see you, and I hoped we could start over."

"I'm sure we can!" declared Vikki, beating back doubts about what Mom would say. "Come inside."

"I'm not interrupting anything?"

"Not really." The sounds of the spanking stopped. A thud shook the floor as Nikki jumped off Mom's lap. "Nikki—my little sister—and Mom and I were just going to sit down for supper. There's enough to go around."

"Little sister? Is Monica married again?" Dad hesitated in the hall.

"She was. He left," said Vikki shortly. "Mom—"

Nikki appeared in the living-room doorway. "Who's that?"

Mom appeared behind her. "Oh, my!"

"Dad, this is Nikki Studer, my baby sister," said Vikki, wondering what Mom's expression meant. "Nikki, this is my daddy. Dave Baum."

"*Your* daddy?" Nikki sounded—what? Offended? "You don't have a daddy!"

"She sure does," said Dad, "and I'm it." He reached down his hand, shake-fashion. "You can call me Uncle Dave."

Nikki put her hands behind her back. "What if I don't want to?"

Vikki felt her face turn red.

Mom pushed Nikki. "Behave yourself for once, can't you? Hi, Dave."

"Hi, Monica. It's good to see you again."

"You won't believe this, but it's good to see you again, too," said Mom slowly. "You should've been here a long time ago. And I'm not talking about eleven years' worth of child support, neither!" She twisted her neck, rubbing the place where she was always stiff from holding the phone to her ear. "Though you can't expect me to forget all about that in a minute, either. I don't know what to say."

"I do," said Nikki. "I'm hungry."

"And dinner's on the table," added Vikki hastily. "Come eat with us."

"Okay," said Dad. "Thanks."

Vikki felt her heart swelling as she led him to the kitchen, knowing her life would never be the same after this, and wondering eagerly exactly how it would change.

THREE

Nikki Acts Like a Little Pill

NIKKI SPENT DINNER PLAYING WITH HER FOOD, PUTTING her elbows on the table, humming, and getting jabbed and glared at by Mom. Vikki didn't even notice. She was too busy talking to her dad. Some dad! He had ugly teeth and thin hair. Nikki couldn't remember her own daddy at all, though Mom always made her bless him in her prayers at night, but she bet he was better-looking than this loser! She wouldn't call this guy Uncle Dave, not for a million billion trillion dollars. She mopped melted butter off her plate with her fingers and thought about what she would call him instead, as he and Vikki and Mom laughed over a stupid story he was telling. Dumb Dave. Dorky Dave. Old Brown Teeth.

"So I didn't keep that job long!" Everybody was laughing. Nikki had missed the point of the story, and was sure it wasn't really funny, anyway. "I got out of Houston after that," Old Brown Teeth went on. "That town was just no good to me. But I'm working again now." He looked serious. "I wish I could make it up to you, all those years I didn't send the support checks. It must've been hard on y'all."

Mom and Vikki looked at each other, then Vikki said, "Don't worry about it. We're okay."

"Not that it wouldn't be welcome if you started those payments up now," added Mom, smiling.

Old Brown Teeth nodded. "Sure. Sure. I plan to. And I'll make it up to you as much as I can." He pulled a card out of his breast pocket, with a necklace wrapped around it. "Here's a little tiny start—for you, Vikki. I ran into this guy in a booth at the mall near where I live, and he was making names in gold wire. So I thought, Hey, I bet Vikki never sees her name spelled right."

"Oh, it's gorgeous!" Vikki clapped her hands.

Nikki slumped in her chair till her feet were on the floor and her eyes barely cleared the tabletop. Mom yanked her upright, frowning. Nikki frowned back. She was real tired of Mom always being in a bad mood with her, and in a good mood with everybody else. If Nikki had run off even for a day, she'd have had no supper when she got home, but this guy had been gone for longer than Nikki had been alive, and nobody was punishing him!

Vikki smiled at Old Brown Teeth, looked at Nikki, then looked at the card. "Oh, good. It's got his phone number. Maybe we can get a matching one for Nikki."

Nikki sat up straighter.

"She's too young for something that delicate," said Mom.

Nikki slumped again.

Old Brown Teeth leaned back in his chair. "That's for starters. And I thought we could go out to eat tomorrow night, just you and me, and get acquainted."

"That'd be—" Vikki stopped, and looked at Mom. "I have to stay home and take care of Nikki. Maybe some other time."

"Mrs. Lozano can baby-sit Nikki," said Mom.

"I don't like Mrs. Lozano," grumped Nikki.

"Oh, you do, too." Mom looked at her as if she were guessing her weight. "You look tired. Don't you think it's time you took your bath and went to bed?"

"No," said Nikki, but Mom got up to run the bathwater anyway.

Normally Nikki was an expert at delaying bedtime, but normally Vikki was putting her to bed. Mom was in no mood to put in bubble bath, tell stories, or even sing the bedbug song. Not that Mom ever was in that kind of mood. Nikki lay awake, listening to the laughter beyond the closed door, and not feeling the least bit sleepy. She tried to bite her own big toe, sang to herself, had a conversation with her stuffed pig and her rag doll in which they all agreed that Old Brown Teeth stank, and chewed her fingernails. Three times she heard a car and looked out the window to check on it. The first time it was Old Baldy leaving; the second time it was Old Baldy coming back. In the light from the back porch she could see him carrying a big plastic box with holes in it and a handle. Howls came from the box. He must be bringing his cat back from the vet. She didn't sound happy to be home. After that Nikki had to listen to the cat as well as to the laughter.

The third time she heard a car, she looked out and

couldn't see anything through the window. It must have been Old Brown Teeth leaving, though, because soon the bathwater started running, and Vikki came in for her robe. "What are you doing still awake?" she asked.

"It's not my fault," said Nikki. "Mom put me to bed too early."

"It wasn't as early as you think," said Vikki. "We had a late dinner." She stroked Nikki's hair and yawned. "Lie down and try to sleep, okay? I won't be long."

Nikki lay down till Vikki closed the door, then sat up again, waiting. As soon as she heard Vikki's footsteps return to the door, she lay down again. "I tried, but I couldn't sleep."

Vikki sighed. "Did you count sheep?"

"That doesn't work. Tell me a story."

"I'm too tired to tell stories." Vikki slung her robe onto the foot of the bed. "How about the bedbug song?"

Nikki nodded. Vikki made her fingers into tiny legs, starting at Nikki's head and marching down her length, singing:

"Onward, marching bedbugs,
Marching down the sheet!
When you reach the bottom
Don't you...tickle my feet!"

Nikki squealed as the legs turned into tickling hands. They thrashed about for a few seconds, then Vikki lay down, and kissed Nikki's forehead. "Good night, Nikki."

"Good night, Vikki."

They lay quiet until Nikki had a sudden, wonderful

thought. "Maybe my daddy'll come back tomorrow," she said.

"Oh, Nikki!" Vikki sounded sad. "Don't count on it."

"If yours can, mine can," said Nikki stoutly. "And mine won't have brown teeth, either."

Vikki was quiet for a long time. "Anything's possible," she said, "but good things always come as a surprise. So try not to expect it, okay? That could make it not happen." She rolled over.

In Old Baldy's apartment, the cat hissed and howled.

Nikki's daddy did not come to see her the next day, or the next, or the next.

Vikki's daddy did, though. He took Vikki to dinner on Saturday, went to church with the family Sunday, and took Vikki shopping for a new swimsuit on Monday. Saturday he brought Nikki a coloring book, which she refused to color in.

Most afternoons, Vikki and Nikki would walk to the public pool, where Vikki sat in a deck chair in her new yellow one-piece, talking to Mando Gonzalez and other people from her high school. Nikki played in the crowded water with the other kids from the neighborhood, and usually forgot that she was having a bad summer. Mornings, Vikki did housework and practiced her violin, and Nikki looked for something to do. The problem was, the only other kid her age on the block was that tattletale Rudy, and she wasn't allowed to go more than a block by herself. She couldn't convince Vikki she was big enough to go farther than that alone. "There aren't going to be any more kidnappers on Mary Ellen's block than on this one," she griped to Vikki.

"But I can hear you scream if they grab you on this block," said Vikki.

"Not if you're practicing the violin."

"Give it a rest, Nikki!"

So Nikki had to invent things to do, and got into trouble, unless she could fib her way out. She usually managed, if there were no witnesses, since Mom wasn't around. Vikki gave her the benefit of the doubt whenever she could, but Mom took it for granted that Nikki was always lying.

Evenings, after Mom was home and dinner eaten and the dishes washed, they'd play Aggravation or watch TV—unless Old Brown Teeth came over. Weekends he came over a lot, always polite and smiling and hateful. He took them to Splashtown, where Nikki was too short to ride the slides and had to spend most of her time in the kiddie-park section. He bought nice things for Vikki, and slightly-less-nice things for Nikki, which she wouldn't use unless Vikki made her. It would've been a great summer without him, because Mom's new boyfriend, Andy, bought them things, too—ice-cream cones and Avon jewelry.

Besides going to the pool every day, the only good thing was Old Baldy's cat, Fuzzface.

Fuzzface was locked up in the house, crying off and on, for days. Old Baldy had blocked shut the hole in the top of his closet, but he told Vikki when she asked that Fuzzface had lost half her tail and was wearing a big round collar that kept her from picking at her bandages. When she finally came out, she didn't look the way Nikki remembered her—a fluffy, high-stepping silver cat with a gray tail carried straight in the air. Instead, she walked close to the ground, with her short tail carried low behind her.

Vikki was practicing her violin. Nikki was sitting on the back porch playing jacks with herself when the scruffy black cat that raided the garbage came into the yard and walked up to Fuzzface, who was enjoying the sun on the porch rail. He hopped right up onto the rail and walked toward her, walking as if he took up more space than he really did. Fuzzface laid her ears back and growled at him, jerking her silly-looking short tail. Scruffy kept coming, turning his ears around, the hair on his spine standing up. Fuzzface started to back away.

"Hey!" Nikki stood up. Both cats froze. "That isn't fair," she said. "It's Fuzzface's porch."

"Grr," said Scruffy, watching her as she came to stand next to Fuzzface.

"*Grr* yourself," said Nikki. She took a step toward him and shooed him with her hands. He backed up then, as she kept coming toward him, and hopped down from the porch rail and ran off. "There," said Nikki. "That'll show him he can't boss you around just 'cause your tail's short."

Fuzzface looked after him, then started to wash her quivering fur. Nikki went back to playing jacks. After a while Fuzzface hopped down and started playing with her, only she changed the rules, batting the jacks around the porch, and chasing the bouncing ball. It was more fun than the regular way, and the two of them were still playing when Old Baldy came home.

Fuzzface ran up to him and rubbed against his ankles. "Y'all having a good time?" he asked.

Nikki nodded, feeling slightly nervous; but he didn't seem to remember that she'd ever been bad to him. He reached into his pocket and pulled out two sticks of Doublemint gum, gave her one, and took the other himself. "Good," he said, petting the cat. "Having her tail cut off traumatized her something awful. The anesthetic they gave her made her have hallucinations, and she hated the collar. It's about time poor Fuzzface had some fun."

"What's traumatized?" Nikki asked.

"When something horrible happens to you and you can't get over it," said Old Baldy. "Only most people do get over it, eventually. It just takes a lot of hard work. Fuzzface didn't lose any of your jacks for you, did she?"

"I didn't have them all to start with, anyway," said Nikki. She kind of liked the way Old Baldy was talking to her, as if she were a normal human being the same as him, and not some pesky kid. She liked the gum, too. And she liked it that Fuzzface started coming out to play with her every time she played with something small enough to chase or bat around.

Other than little things like that, it was the worst summer of her whole entire life, and it was all Old Brown Teeth's fault.

FOUR

Vikki Enjoys Herself and Others

IT WAS THE BEST SUMMER OF VIKKI'S LIFE SO FAR.

She practiced her violin daily, feeling herself getting better—able to catch not just the notes, but the spirit of the music. She went to Mando Gonzalez's house one evening with a wad of sheet music, and they played "the composer's challenge," sight-reading pieces they had never seen before, whether designed for their instruments (Mando was the orchestra's percussion section) or not. It ended with them both paralyzed with laughter on his garage floor. Afterward Mando said she was a shoo-in for first-chair violin and a music scholarship.

Mando had never noticed her before this summer, though Vikki had noticed him—not good-looking, but competent and unflustered, playing the drums and cymbals, triangle and bells, all by himself in the back of the orchestra. Nobody else in the school realized the musical potential of percussion; they just wanted something to bang on so that they could be in parades and tramp around the football field at halftime.

Vikki felt almost that she was magic, and she knew she was slim and healthy (had she ever looked as good in her life as she did in her new yellow swimsuit?), efficient and creative. Every meal she cooked was perfect, it seemed to her, and even dusting and sweeping and picking up after Nikki were jobs performed quickly and well. Resentment at having to do all the housework, irritation with Mom's ways of doing things, impatience with Nikki's mishaps— all the feelings she normally had to work to keep inside seemed to go away.

Vikki could date the beginning of the magic, too. The evening her dad came back, something marvelous had happened, as if her life had been twisted out of shape, and his return straightened everything out. She hadn't been aware of missing him, or anything like that—though she had sometimes tried to fit together her bits of memories (riding on his back in the kiddie pool, giggling uncontrollably as he tickled her) with the fact of his absence. What sort of man could tuck a little girl into bed with the bedbug song, and then vanish forever? It made no sense—and she no longer had to try to make sense of it, because he was no longer gone forever. Mom was right, after all. Despite all the evidence, fathers loved their children. Maybe Nikki's dad *would* come back, too, someday.

Not that Dad was perfect; but he had taken steps to correct his greatest fault, and both Vikki and Mom were inclined to forgive him the rest. Other people were sterner. "So has he paid you any child support yet?" Mom's new boyfriend, Andy, asked one night when they had him over for dinner. He and Mom were sitting on the back porch afterward, and Vikki was coming out to bring them cold drinks after putting Nikki to bed.

"Not yet," said Mom. "I don't even remember what he was supposed to pay."

"Has anybody tried to find out?"

Vikki stepped onto the porch as Mom answered, "After eleven years, what's the rush?"

"After eleven years, what's the holdup?" asked Andy. "You could use some of that money."

"He was unemployed for a while," said Vikki. "Give him time to get caught up." Mom glanced from Vikki to Andy, and Vikki made her tone softer, handing Andy a glass (already sweating). "He came back. That's the main thing."

That was all that was said about it at the time, though the atmosphere was always uncomfortable when Dad and Andy were in the same room. Vikki tried to keep them apart, and refused to think about it. She didn't like Andy much herself, but Mom was always happy around him, and that was what mattered.

Mom's being happy was another wonderful part of the summer. She and Andy went out every weekend, and every day of the week she fussed with her makeup and laughed a lot. She was always like this when she got a new boyfriend. Even Nikki's fits of naughtiness didn't make her as mad as usual.

But Nikki was naughty often. She would slip outside and hide under the porch or in the crape myrtle when bedtime got near. She served herself Kool-Aid in glass

27

tumblers when she was supposed to use plastic, and the day she broke one, she cleaned it up and hid the pieces, lying when confronted with the evidence. She ignored the gifts Dad brought her, was rude to Mrs. Lozano when Vikki's and Mom's going out at the same time made a baby-sitter necessary, and was an all-around little pill. Vikki felt sorry for her, though. She was so obviously jealous of Vikki for having a daddy.

Vikki remembered Nikki's dad clearly, though he'd left when she was nine and Nikki was two weeks old. He'd been as bad as no dad at all—seldom employed, frequently drunk, and not interested enough in his little girl to play with her or help take care of her. She suspected that Nikki's bad behavior was inherited from him. There was no point in telling the poor kid that, though. She got enough grief from Mom, and she wasn't trying to be naughty. Things just happened that way when she tried to do things for herself, that was all. Often Vikki thought Mom was too strict with her—but it wasn't her place to say so. Mom counted on Vikki to back her up, and Vikki wasn't about to let her down.

One windless August day Vikki and Nikki came back from the pool to find Dad's battered green Dodge parked in front of the house and Dad waiting on the front porch, talking to Mr. Grant and idly whittling at the porch rail with his Buck knife. The men broke off their conversation as Vikki hurried up, fishing the key out of the pocket of her shorts.

"Daddy! Hi! What're you doing over here so early?"

"I went to work at six to meet an early shipment," said Dad, "so they let me go at three. Thought I'd take my girl to dinner and a movie."

Dad still hadn't paid any child support, but Vikki suppressed that thought as she unlocked the door. "That'd be great—but I'm already going out tonight." Vikki looked at Nikki, who had hung back and was talking to Mr. Grant while glaring at Dad.

"Oh? Not that Mexican boy?"

Dad and Mando had met only once. Vikki didn't know why Dad had to call him "that Mexican boy," but she wasn't going to make an issue of it. It wasn't as if she planned to get married or anything. "Mando, yes," she said, stepping inside and motioning to Nikki. "His big brother's working at this *conjunto* club that gets all the hot groups, and he's going to get us in."

"Con-hoon-to?" Exaggerating the Spanish pronunciation, Dad followed her in. Nikki trailed behind reluctantly. "What d'you want to listen to that trash for? Thought you were into classical stuff—Bach, and those people."

"Music's music, Daddy!" Vikki used a phrase out of a music review that she had liked: "*Conjunto*'s the 'authentic spirit of South Texas,' and I'm an authentic South Texan. Besides, we might get to go backstage." She took Nikki's bundle of towels and swimsuit, and noticed her jaws working. "What're you chewing?"

Nikki opened her mouth to reveal a purple wad on a purple tongue. "Grape gum. Old Baldy gave it to me."

"Don't call Mr. Grant Old Baldy! It's rude."

"Didn't Monica teach you girls not to take stuff from men?" asked Dad.

"Strangers," said Nikki, "not men!"

"Mr. Grant's okay, Dad!" Vikki went through the kitchen and unlocked the back door. "And Mando's okay, and you don't have to worry about us." She carried the towels and wet swimsuits onto the back porch, hanging them over the rail to dry. Mr. Grant's cat, Fuzzface, ran away to hide in the crape myrtle.

"I don't know; maybe I fuss too much," said Dad, trailing after her. "But I worry about you. Mr. Grant seems okay, but what do you really know about him? And this Mando boy—what kind of guy takes an underage girl to a bar?"

"It's not a bar, it's a club, and his brother's letting us in on condition we only buy Cokes." Vikki smiled teasingly. "You're jealous 'cause you wanted to take me out tonight."

"You got me there!" Dad laughed. "Tell you what, though—I get off at noon on Fridays. Whyn't we go somewhere in the afternoon? You got any shopping to do?"

"School starts in a couple of weeks, but I won't know how much I can spend on clothes till Mom pays bills." Vikki knew that she'd probably have to go to Goodwill again this year, but she wasn't going to whine to Dad about it.

"Who said you had to spend anything?" Dad patted her shoulder. "I'll take you to the mall and we'll go hog-wild with my paycheck. How's that?"

"What about Nikki? Mom won't be home till almost six."

"Get Mrs. Lozano to watch her."

"Well...It's kind of short notice, but I'll ask." There wouldn't be any problem with Mom. Dad buying her school clothes would be a big relief on the budget, so Mom would be thrilled. "I'll go ahead and call Mrs. Lozano now. If she can't do it tomorrow, how about Saturday?"

"Whatever," said Dad.

Mrs. Lozano grumbled a little about the short notice, but agreed to watch Nikki if Vikki gave her her lunch first; and Mom, when she came home, was as pleased as if Dad had written her a check. "Actual new clothes for school! What a concept!" Mom grinned, helping herself to the chili Vikki had made for supper.

"Does that mean I get new clothes, too?" asked Nikki, crumbling her corn bread instead of eating it.

"Sure," said Vikki, at the same time that Mom said, "I'm not sure there's any point getting new clothes for you. You grow so darn fast! And you're so hard on them anyway."

Nikki's lower lip poked out.

"I've got an idea," said Vikki. "Why don't I drag out that old portable sewing machine in the back of your closet, Mom? Nikki and I can go to Fabric Warehouse and pick out patterns and material, and I can make her clothes with plenty of room to let out when she grows."

"That's an awful big job," warned Mom.

"I can help," said Nikki eagerly.

"It won't be so bad," said Vikki. "Remember when I took home ec, how fast I made that dress?"

"Well, I won't try to stop you," said Mom. "It would be nice to send her out looking civilized for once."

Nikki wiggled in her chair. "We could pick out material tomorrow."

"Vikki's daddy's taking her shopping tomorrow," said Mom.

"So? I could go, too."

"You weren't invited."

"We'll go Saturday; I promise," Vikki put in hastily.

Nikki glowered, but let the subject hang till after supper, when she followed Vikki back to the bedroom and watched her get ready for her date. "How come you're always going out these days?" she asked, sitting on the bed with her chin on her knees.

"Just lucky, I guess," said Vikki absently, carefully stroking on her eye shadow. Should she shop for make-up tomorrow, too? Maybe if the drugstore in the mall had a sale—

"It's no fair," said Nikki. "You and Mom get to go on dates all the time, and I never do."

"Little girls don't go on dates," said Vikki, glossing her lips. "Wait a few years. You'll have as many dates as you can handle."

"I don't see why I can't go with you and Old Brown Teeth tomorrow."

Vikki turned sharply. "*What* did you call him?"

Nikki chewed her knee.

Vikki faced the mirror again, glancing at the clock. Ten minutes! She wished she could just throw Nikki out and get ready in peace; but being patient was part of the big-sister job. She took a deep breath and summoned up some good advice, leaning closer to the mirror to make sure everything went on straight. "You know, you'd have a better time if you'd think less about yourself and more about other people. If you'd try being sweet to them, and thinking about what they want instead of what you want, they'd like to be around you, and you wouldn't be so grumpy all the time."

"I don't know how." Nikki dropped over sideways, looking at Vikki from under an outstretched arm. "I try and I try and it all gets messed up and I get mad and I forget. Anyway, why should I? Nobody thinks about what I want."

"That's not true! Mom and I do."

"You do sometimes. Mom doesn't."

"Sure she does! But you fight her so much you never notice."

Nikki made a rude noise, but Vikki didn't have time to mess with her anymore, and it was too small a thing to bother Mom with.

FIVE

Nikki Sneaks Along

VIKKI'S RETURN IN THE SMALL HOURS OF THE MORNING woke Nikki, but only barely.

Vikki usually got up to fix breakfast when Mom started running the shower, but today she only rolled over, so Nikki decided she would try, really try, to be sweet and helpful and think of others. She went to the kitchen. Cereal would be easiest to fix, but Vikki always made Mom scrambled eggs, so that would be most thoughtful.

Unfortunately Mom came in just as the eggs hissed into the smoking melted butter, before Nikki had a chance to pick up the spatula she'd dropped on the floor or wipe up the egg white that had gotten on the counter. Mom shouted, "What do you think you're doing?" as she turned down the gas on the burner.

"Making breakfast," said Nikki. Mom was clearly very angry, so she lied at once: "Vikki told me to."

"Vikki's still asleep!" Mom put her hands on her hips and stood over Nikki, who stepped back.

"She went back to sleep after she said that," Nikki invented.

"Oh, right!" Mom glared around the room. "Look at this mess! You know you're not allowed to play with fire!"

"I wasn't playing," said Nikki. "I was cooking."

Vikki came in, blinking. "What's the ruckus?"

Vikki seemed to understand, despite both of them talking at once; but she couldn't calm Mom down, and the upshot was that Nikki was spanked and sent to her room till lunchtime, vowing never ever ever to be good again.

"I know you didn't mean to be naughty," Vikki said, letting her out the minute lunch was ready—eleven o'clock, a whole hour earlier than usual. "You have got to learn to think before you do things. Stoves are dangerous—especially when you're little."

"I'm not so little. I'm almost in fourth grade." Nikki climbed into her chair and glared at lunch—hot dogs and french fries, her favorite.

"You have to be in middle school before you can use a stove," said Vikki firmly. "Eat up, or there won't be time to play before Dad comes."

As soon as the dishes were rinsed they went outside to play. The wagon was a boat that sailed all around the front yard before wrecking itself on the front steps. Vikki, as captain, went down with her ship, temporarily became a helpful monkey on a desert island where Nikki was cast away, and finally transformed into the captain of a passing steamer, to whom Nikki signaled with a mirror. "Long long long, short short short, long long long," she repeated to herself, moving the mirror to catch the sunlight as Vikki had shown her. "What does that mean?"

"It's Morse code for SOS," said Vikki. "Anytime you're in trouble, you can signal that, and they'll understand you all over the world."

"But what does it *mean*?"

"'Save our skins,' I think. Where should my ship be from?"

"Africa," said Nikki. "You're carrying monkeys and parrots for the circus."

Before Vikki could get back to her boat, Old Brown Teeth drove up and honked. Vikki waved to him, but he didn't get out. "Is there anything you want to take to Mrs. Lozano's?" she asked Nikki, taking back her mirror.

Nikki folded her arms. "Ask him if I can go, too. He'll do it, if you ask him."

"I'll do no such thing! You behave yourself." Vikki walked to the car, Nikki trailing after. Inside, the car was a mess—you couldn't even see the backseat. "I'll be a minute," Vikki said to Old Brown Teeth. "I've got to lock up and take Nikki to Mrs. Lozano's."

Old Brown Teeth sighed impatiently and switched off the car. "You know, you could've done all that before," he said. "I'll help you lock up. And Nikki can take herself to Mrs. Lozano's." He got out, leaving his door unlocked.

"I'm going, I'm going," Nikki said before anyone could tell her to leave. She hugged Vikki.

"I'll be back in time to make supper," said Vikki, hugging back. "Tomorrow we'll do your shopping. Promise."

Nikki ran down the street to Mrs. Lozano's house, and onto the porch. Before ringing the doorbell, she looked over her shoulder. Vikki and Old Brown Teeth were going inside. She pushed the bell three times rapidly, and Mrs. Lozano came to the door. "All right! All right! Keep your hair on!"

"Hi," said Nikki. "I came to tell you you don't have to baby-sit me today. Vikki's dad said I could go with him."

Mrs. Lozano looked happy. "I don't know why y'all couldn't've planned to do that in the first place," she said. "You have a good time."

"Okay." Nikki ran back to the car and glanced around before she opened the door. Inside, she crawled over the driver's seat and dropped down to the floor among McDonald's bags, old clothes, and mysterious pieces of machinery. It was a tight fit, and the car smelled sour, but Nikki rearranged Old Brown Teeth's junk until she fit, her head against the front passenger seat, her feet on the hump, her shoulder blades against the door. A dirty old quilt, hastily draped, hid her from above.

Nikki's neck started to hurt, and she had to change her position twice, before Vikki and Old Brown Teeth got into the car. "I'm just saying you've got to be careful around those boys," Old Brown Teeth said, slamming his door as Vikki fastened her seat belt. "If you want to get involved in that sort of thing, wait for the guy that loves you."

"Oh, Daddy! Mando and I aren't going to do anything like that!" Vikki laughed.

"Bet that's not what he's thinking," said Old Brown Teeth, starting the car.

Down on the floor, the engine noise was loud enough to drown out most of what else they said. Nikki stared at the quilt pattern and planned how she would reveal herself.

She'd wait till they were in the mall parking lot, and then she'd sit up and yell, "Surprise!" Vikki would be mad, of course, and Nikki would probably get a spanking when Mom found out, too.

The sound of the car changed as they got onto the highway. "This isn't the way to the mall," said Vikki.

"Thought we'd go over to Westlakes Mall, near where I live," said Old Brown Teeth. "And while I've got you on that side of town, there's this place Monica and I used to go that I wanted to show you, between here and Castroville."

"That's kind of a long ride, isn't it?" Vikki turned on the radio.

"It'll be worth it."

Vikki fiddled with the radio knob till she found her classical music station. Some of the stuff Vikki practiced was okay, but all those wordless notes coming out of the radio bored Nikki stiff. Vikki and Old Brown Teeth kept talking, but Nikki could only understand a word here and there.

Without noticing it, she fell asleep.

Nikki woke to silence, unable to breathe in the heat beneath the quilt. She sat up, fighting her way through a layer of trash. The car was stopped, and Vikki and Old Brown Teeth were already gone. Nikki scrambled onto the backseat, her hand on the door—and stopped, puzzled. This wasn't the mall!

This wasn't anywhere. Nikki looked around at heat-yellowed grass and dull-green clumps of trees. Far away, big silver towers slung with power lines marched along the horizon. The car was parked at a lopsided gate. Some distance away stood a house, mostly held together by trumpet vine. Locusts clustered thickly on the gatepost, their buzzing swelling and fading.

As Nikki tried to make sense of this view, a harsh, shrill sound split the locust buzz. What on earth—? Nikki climbed onto the back of the driver's seat and stuck her head out the open window, listening. Some animal, maybe? It sounded kind of like the screams she'd heard on TV, only rougher, and all broken up. Deep scream, shrill scream, silence. Shaky scream, silence. It occurred to Nikki that it would be possible to scream SOS in Morse code, but this had no pattern. It was just interrupted noise. After a while it stopped altogether.

Nikki looked at the clock on the dashboard. Two-seventeen—not quite an hour since they'd left home. She was thinking of getting out and looking around when the house door opened and Old Brown Teeth hurried out, letting the door bang shut behind him. He'd spilled something dark all over his shirt. Nikki ducked behind the seat and pulled the quilt over her. The world narrowed to a view between the seat and the car door.

The door opened. Something small and dark fell as Old Brown Teeth got in, breathing hard. As he slammed the door shut, he swore, the same bad word three or four times in a row, his voice shaking. "Stupid girl," he said. "I can't believe this! Well, it's her own fault!"

Nikki's back itched, but she didn't dare move as he swore some more. After a while the car started. The radio came on at the same time, lively fiddle music dancing out of the speakers for a few seconds before Old Brown Teeth

39

swore again and switched it off. The seat creaked and pressed hard against Nikki as he settled back in it, turned the car around, and drove. Nikki braced herself against the floor, trying not to be shaken around. How had she slept through this the first time? Maybe he hadn't been going so fast.

And where was Vikki?

Old Brown Teeth drove a long, long time on the bouncy road, taking turns too fast and sometimes swearing some more. Finally, after a large bump that pushed Nikki so roughly into the back of the seat that she was sure he had to feel it, the sound and the motion changed. They were back on a paved road. Shortly Old Brown Teeth slowed down and changed direction, driving into shade and stopping. He got out and hurried away. She heard a door open and shut.

Nikki poked her head up. The car was parked in front of the rest room on the side of a Conoco station. A yellow dog sprawled in the shade of the red-painted brick wall, and an old woman pumped gas for herself at the front of the station. The road was some sort of highway. She could see the white Texas shape on the black road sign, but not the number. She could also see a couple of houses, a trailer, and an overpass. She was beginning to get nervous about hiding in the car, but if she got out here, she'd never find her way home again.

Nikki tried to hide more comfortably, but she didn't have many options. After a while footsteps came around the building, and the dog greeted someone. "Hi, Lady," said a boy's voice. Whoever it was knocked on the rest-room door.

"It's taken!" yelled Old Brown Teeth.

"Okay." The voice went back to the dog, talking pet talk to her. Old Brown Teeth didn't come out, and didn't come out. The person waiting knocked again. "You drowning in there?"

Old Brown Teeth swore some more.

"Come on! I got to get back to the register!" said the boy.

Nikki heard the rest-room door. "All right, all right!"

"It's about time, mister! It looks like you took a bath in there!" The door shut again.

Old Brown Teeth got back into the car and started driving.

When they finally reached town and got off the highway, Old Brown Teeth had to slow down and take more corners. After he stopped and got out, rolling up the windows and locking the door, Nikki lay still as long as she could stand to.

This time, she was in the carport of a two-story pink building, probably apartments. The dashboard clock told her it was almost four o'clock. No one seemed to be around. She unlocked the door, let herself out, and locked it again. The lot gave directly onto a street, its baked blacktop swelling and glittering in the August sunlight. Nikki walked to the corner and looked at the sign, but she had never heard of either street.

Her stomach started to hurt.

SIX

Vikki Helps Herself

WHEN VIKKI WAS CERTAIN HER FATHER WAS GONE, SHE let out her breath in a long, gasping sob. Weak and sick and hurting worse than she had known how to hurt, she dragged herself out from under the steel sink, into the dappled light that the trumpet-vine-curtained windows let in. One of her contact lenses had come out, leaving the world fuzzy and lopsided. The tears didn't help, either.

The stab wound in Vikki's leg was still bleeding. Thick red liquid pulsed silently on her thigh, tears poured down her face, and she would have felt much better if she could have thrown up. But somewhere in the core of her brain something calm told her hands what to do.

The cotton skirts of both sundress and slip were bloody and torn where the knife had gone through. It was easy to tear them further, get rid of the dirtiest parts, and make raggedy bandages. Working as steadily as she could through waves of nausea and darkness, Vikki tightly wrapped her leg above the wound, the picture of the tourniquet in last year's health textbook surprisingly clear in her mind.

She should have a stick. Fumbling on the floor, she picked up her rat-tail comb, lying where it had spilled when Dad first hit her and she had dropped her purse. The comb tail was short and thin, but when she twisted the cloth with it, as the tourniquet picture had shown, it tightened the bandage better than she could have done without it. When the leg began to feel numb, she untwisted it. When she saw the blood try to run out again, she tightened it.

All the time, tears poured down her face and her throat ached from crying. Vikki could hear herself saying, "No no no it didn't happen no no no." She couldn't stop, and the dimness of the room seemed to rise up and drown her.

For a long time after the darkness passed Vikki lay listening to the flies buzz, her eyes closed. She had several small cuts, but only the one on her thigh was deep. Her head ached where it had hit the sink. And she had too many small aches and bruises to keep track of, plus one particularly nauseating pain in her side.

Dad must be crazy, Vikki thought. She should have realized something was wrong when she'd found out the special place he was taking her to was where he and Mom had used to go to make out. Normal dads didn't do that. She hadn't realized he was crazy, though. She had decided to go back to the car, and he had blocked her way, and that was when the craziness kicked in. He must have lost eighteen years of his life, mistaken her for Mom, and decided they had come here to make out.

But then why had Dad kept calling her Vikki as he tried to make her kiss him?

And why had he beaten her up so badly, when she wouldn't?

And what if he came back?

I don't deserve this, Vikki thought, opening her eyes and waving the tickling flies off her smaller, unbandaged cuts. Already the places where she had bled on the floor swarmed with flies. The sight brought her closer to throwing up than she'd been yet; but she still didn't. The flies she shooed away circled and landed again.

Vikki stood carefully, wincing at the pain in her side and then in her leg. She had stopped crying, but her head still ached, and with her lopsided vision it was hard to decide what she was looking at. She got her contact lens case off the floor, took the remaining lens out of her eye, and put on her glasses. Mechanically, she started to sort the rest of her scattered belongings—mirror, manicure set, pizza coupons, contacts solution, gum, coin purse, billfold, datebook, pencil—into the compartments of her purse, but it suddenly seemed pointless. She couldn't imagine why she had ever bothered. Scooping everything up in handfuls, she filled her purse and got her bearings.

The steel sink had a pump handle instead of a faucet. Vikki hoped this meant it was hooked up to a well instead of to a water main. Any city water the house had once been entitled to would have been cut off years ago. The handle moved stiffly, but she couldn't tell if the drag on the upstroke was the result of rust or of climbing water.

Pumping hurt, pulling at the sorest spot in her side, but

Vikki knew nothing else to do. If Dad was crazy...It made no difference, except that, if he came back, she would have to hide from him. She was hurt and she wasn't sure where she was—someplace between San Antonio and Castroville. No one but her father knew where to find her. All she could see through the window over the sink was prairie and trees. If she stayed here, she would starve, or (the pump handle creaked and groaned and dragged at all the muscles in her upper body) die of thirst, or catch some horrible disease from the flies. She had to find her own way back to civilization.

Vikki prayed in time to the motion of the pump handle. There had to be water down there, didn't there? She had read something about "pump priming" once. Pouring water in from the top was supposed to help bring water up from the bottom, though she wasn't sure how that worked. She got her bottle of contact solution, the only liquid she had. Squirting from the little nozzle resulted in only a thin thread of liquid, and taking the lid off and try-ing to pour it up the down-pointing spout lost her most of it. Vikki blinked back tears of pain and frustration as she pumped. If she got all the way through saying "The Lord is My Shepherd" without getting any water, she'd give up and do...something else.

On "I shall fear no evil," she felt a change in the stiffness of the pump. Finishing the psalm in a mindless gabble, Vikki pumped harder, gasping and grunting with the effort. The pump gurgled, choked, and spat tea-colored water into the sink. Vikki pushed herself to keep pumping till the water ran clear and white, and then was afraid to stop. She got a warm drink as she pumped by bending her head; but what if the water stopped when her arms did and ran all the way back down the pipe and wouldn't come up again? She pushed the worst of the dirt in the sink down the drain with one hand, considering.

She hooked the purse with her foot and lifted it up off the floor. Letting go of the pump with one hand and continuing to work the handle with the other, she dug out her coin purse. It didn't quite plug the drain, but it slowed the water's exit enough that, by pumping quickly, she nearly filled the sink.

Vikki washed as best she could. The wound on her leg had stopped bleeding, but she rinsed out her improvised bandage and tied it back on. Though warm to taste, the water turned cool soon after it touched her skin. She began to feel better.

Retrieving her coin purse so that the dirty water could run out, Vikki wandered around the house, looking out the other windows. The house had been empty so long that it didn't even feel abandoned; it was more like an arbor than a house. Through the windows she could see trumpet vine, with hummingbirds blurring between the long orange flowers. It took an effort of will to focus past that. More prairies, more stands of live oak, and silver towers holding power lines against the deepening blue sky.

How late was it? Vikki went outside, where an evening breeze stirred on her skin. The nausea of her hurts was fading, and she was beginning to get hungry. I guess I should just follow the road, she thought.

But what if Dad came back?

She'd be able to see the car coming from a long way away, and hide in the grass.

Vikki shaded her eyes. She could see a long way, but she couldn't see the shining movement that would indicate cars on a highway. She couldn't see any signs of buildings. What if darkness came with her still out here?

Vikki sat down on the porch. The boards settled beneath her. She didn't want to start walking right now. Just staying awake was almost more effort than she felt able to make. But if Dad came back, and she was asleep in the house...She had to hide—like Nikki, hiding from trouble.

Poor Nikki—no one to hunt her out from under the porch and take her to bed, singing the bedbug song. Mom was always too tired to sing. Mom would be in a bad mood, anyway, worrying about Vikki. Vikki knew she should be upset about that, but she was worn out, and had the feeling she had almost thought of something. Worry, Mom, bad mood, Nikki, bedtime, hiding—under the porch.

Vikki made herself step down from the porch and walk around it. Sure enough, the latticework on the sides had rotted badly. Vikki broke it easily, making a big enough space to crawl through. Underneath, the dirt was uncomfortable, and would get her cuts dirty, but she didn't care. She hurt too much to crawl out.

Vikki curled up till she was almost as small as Nikki, put her head on her arms, and lay still.

SEVEN

Nikki Gets Home Second

NIKKI PICKED A DIRECTION AND STARTED WALKING, wishing she'd stayed at Mrs. Lozano's. She'd be watching cartoons right now if she had.

A Stop-N-Go store stood on a busy corner, looking so much like the one near home that Nikki felt a rush of hope. The street and surroundings did not get any more familiar as she got closer, though. At least she'd be able to ask the cash-register person where she was. People in stores didn't count as strangers; it wasn't dangerous to talk to them. She began making up stories, in case she needed them, and went in.

Nikki waited while the woman at the register served a couple of people, then went to the counter and said, "Excuse me. Where am I?"

"Stop-N-Go," said the woman. "What you need?"

"I need to know where I am," said Nikki. "I *know* it's a Stop-N-Go."

"Are you lost?"

Nikki wished the woman would just answer. "Probably," she said. "I think I got on the wrong bus. Is it far to Brackenridge Park from here?" If she could get to Brackenridge Park, she could get home. She'd been there on the bus with Vikki a few times.

"Brackenridge Park's clear across town." The woman turned away to help a man with a six-pack of beer. "You better call your mom to come get you."

"She's at work," said Nikki. "Where is it from here? What bus do I take?"

"I don't know, kid! Call somebody."

"You're trying to get to Brackenridge Park?" A man who had been getting a soda squatted down to her level. "You'd have to go downtown and change buses. What are you doing out alone?"

This was a real stranger, not a store person—but the store person wasn't being very helpful. "I wasn't supposed to be," Nikki said. "My sitter got sick, so I need to get to Brackenridge Park where my aunt is."

"I bet that's one sitter you never see again," said the man. "Look, it's a little out of my way, but I could drive you."

Nikki shook her head vigorously. "No. I'm not supposed to take rides from strangers."

It took some arguing—the man had all kinds of ideas about how to track her mom and aunt down by phone, and she had to claim to know nobody's phone number or workplace in the whole world—but he finally walked out with her, showed her the bus stop, and explained to her what to do to get the right bus for Brackenridge Park once she got downtown. Then he made her check how much money she had, and when she only had a nickel, gave her twenty cents for the bus, plus another twenty in case of emergency. Nikki knew she shouldn't take money from strange men, either, but she didn't see how she could get home otherwise, so she did.

Getting home took forever. First, a long, hot wait at the bus stop; then a long bus ride, through parts of town she'd never seen before; then another long, hot wait at a bus stop at a park downtown, clutching the slip of paper that would let her transfer to a new bus without paying; and finally another long bus ride, through streets that eventually looked familiar. By the time she got off at the stop where she and Vikki would wait for the bus to go to Brackenridge Park, she was tired and dying of thirst, had no idea what time it was, and still had to walk five blocks.

Nikki stumped along, hoping Old Baldy or some other nonstranger would offer her a ride. A lot of people drove by, but none of them stopped. If she beat both Vikki and Mom home, she'd be fine. But where had Vikki gone? Had she talked to Mrs. Lozano? And what time was it? Would Mom be on her way yet?

As Nikki turned the corner onto her own street, she saw Mom coming out of Mrs. Lozano's house. Rats! She considered running home and hiding under the porch.

"There you are!" said Mom. "I hope you weren't a big pest, after Dave was nice enough to take you."

"Of course not," said Nikki, crossing the street with her.

"Where's Dave and Vikki?"

"Um...They sent me home on the bus." That was the wrong lie, she knew at once; but it was too late.

Mom looked at her suspiciously. "Vikki wouldn't do that."

"It wasn't her idea." Nikki hopped onto the porch and swung on the rail by her arms.

Mom didn't look convinced, but all she did was open the door and say, "I wonder if I should make Vikki a dinner, or if he's taking her out. I'll wait awhile. They'll call if she's not coming."

But Mom and Nikki watched a whole TV program, and the phone didn't ring. It had been so long since her lunch that Nikki's stomach started growling, so Mom put a frozen pizza into the oven. She kept looking at her watch, then at the phone, and then out the front windows. Bath time came, and still no Vikki.

Mom shoved Nikki into the bathroom. "Don't come out till you're clean," she said, "and believe me, I'll be able to tell!"

Nikki ran her own water, trying to get it the right temperature by turning the hot and cold faucets the way Vikki did. It didn't work. First it was way too cold, and then it was way too hot. She was still trying to get it right, and the tub was getting dangerously full, when Mom came back.

"Oh, for heaven's sake! Why haven't you got in yet?"

"The water's not right."

"It's wet, isn't it?" Mom picked up a hairbrush off the back of the sink. Nikki shut off the water and stepped in. "I just called Dave. He says he didn't take you anywhere."

"Dave's a liar," said Nikki, splashing as she sat down. Ouch! Too hot!

"Where were you all afternoon?"

"Around." Nikki got her horse-shaped soap (no longer very horsy) she'd carved in art class last spring. "Where's Vikki?"

"She ran into one of the Jennifers at the mall and went to a movie with her." Vikki knew three Jennifers. Mom sat down, still fiddling with the hairbrush. "She told Dave she'd call me at work, but I guess she forgot."

"So is she in trouble?" asked Nikki hopefully.

"Never mind that, young lady. Where were you this afternoon? Why'd you lie to Mrs. Lozano and me?"

"I didn't want to go to Mrs. Lozano's," said Nikki.

"So you ran off on your own? What if you'd been kidnapped? Or run over?" Mom put the hairbrush down. "Finish your bath. You're going to bed early tonight. No TV."

Nikki pouted, and took as long as she could washing. She was all wrinkly when she came out, and Mom hustled her straight to bed. She lay awake a long time, listening to the sounds of Old Baldy's model train faintly running next door and woke up three or four times in the night. About midnight she crawled into Vikki's side of the bed, clutching a stuffed animal in each arm. After that she slept better, waking when she heard the shower running in the morning.

Nikki was still on Vikki's side of the bed. Had Vikki slept on Nikki's side, and gotten up already? Nikki leaned over the side of the bed, seeing Vikki's canvas deck shoes still where she'd kicked them off yesterday when putting on her good sandals to go shopping. When she got up and looked, the sandals weren't in their place in the closet, or under the bed. Still holding her pink dog (the oldest and most comforting of her animals), Nikki looked in the kitchen and living room, even in Mom's room.

Mom hurried out of the bathroom, drying her hair.

When she saw Nikki, a hopeful light went out of her face. "Oh, it's you," she said. "I thought I heard Vikki come home."

Nikki shook her head, feeling hollow. "Where is she?"

"I don't know!"

Nikki got down bowls and cereal as Mom went through the list beside the phone, calling all three Jennifers, then Mando Gonzalez, then every other friend Vikki had. The conversations all sounded the same. Nikki sat staring into her bowl of crackling rice, not eating. She felt as if a great big hole had been cut in the world. Mom dialed the phone again.

"Dave? Sorry to wake you, but Vikki isn't home yet....I've called all the Jennifers I know! What was her last name, do you remember?...I don't know that one....No, I guess they could've met at the pool....I called him; I've called everybody!...It's not like her to disappear and not call. She knows I'd be worried....I'm thinking I should call the police....Really? I didn't know that. That's stupid!...Would you? I don't know what we can do, but maybe if we put our heads together....See you in a bit." Mom set down the phone and put her head in her hands.

"What?" asked Nikki. "What's going on?"

"The girl Vikki went off with was named Jennifer Jones," said Mom in a small, tight voice. "I don't know any Jennifer Jones. And Dave says she has to be gone twenty-four hours before the police'll have anything to do with a missing person. That means I can't call them till four o'clock!" Mom rubbed her face, sniffing. "What if she's hurt?"

Nikki sat staring at Mom, hoping she wouldn't cry. She

wanted to cry herself, but she didn't want to make Mom mad. Next door, she heard Old Baldy's back door open.

Leaping to her feet, Nikki ran out onto the back porch just as Fuzzface leaped down the steps and Old Baldy turned the key. "Bal—Mr. Grant!" she cried. "Vikki's gone!"

"Gone?" Old Baldy turned. "Gone how?"

"Nikki, what are you doing?" Mom demanded, coming to the door with her arms folded over her robe.

"Just gone," said Nikki. "She went to a movie and never came back. You're a detective, right? You could find her!"

"Well—" Old Baldy glanced at Mom, and then back at Nikki. "Not without something to go on. Are her clothes still here?"

"She hasn't run away," said Mom. "She wouldn't do that. You're not really a detective, are you?"

"Sure," said Old Baldy. "Missing people aren't what I usually do, but I might be able to save you some trouble here and there. Do you know who she was with? Who saw her last?"

"Some girl I never heard of named Jennifer Jones," said Mom. "She was supposed to drive Vikki home by nine."

"Jennifer Jones. I can remember that. You got a description?"

"I didn't see her. Dave—Vikki's father did. They ran into her up at Windsor Park Mall. And I've called all of Vikki's friends I have phone numbers for."

"Well, if this Jennifer Jones drives, I can probably track her down," said Old Baldy. "My boss has some really neat equipment for invading people's privacy. But I bet you won't need it. Nine times out of ten, when a teenager disappears, she shows up again next day saying, 'Oh, I couldn't get to a phone.'"

"Not Vikki," said Mom. "She'd never do that."

"Give me your phone number," said Old Baldy, "and I'll call you with anything I turn up." He had a little notebook in his pocket, in which Mom wrote the phone number with a shaky hand. Nikki watched him drive away, feeling slightly less empty. A real detective should be able to find Vikki in no time!

EIGHT

Vikki Walks Alone

Vikki slept, dreamed, and woke; slept, dreamed, and woke. The dreams involved kissing Mando, who turned horribly into Dad; muddled battles in which the faces of enemies and allies shifted and changed; and a pursuit through an endless empty house. She woke a final time, stiff and sore and glad to see gray light through the broken latticework of the porch.

Dragging herself out of her hiding place, Vikki brushed the dirt off. Her side hurt so badly that she could only breathe shallowly, and several large, dark bruises had come out on her arms and legs. She had a bump where her head had hit the sink, and the wound on her leg was stiff and sore. But nothing had bled during the night, and most of the nausea and faintness was gone. In the east, the sky was greenish with pink streaks, and no sun yet; but a mockingbird sang his sweet, varied song in the trumpet vine. Vikki went inside.

The pump worked more easily today. Knowing she had nothing to carry water in, Vikki not only washed, but drank as much as she could—much more than she wanted. When she moved she could feel the water sloshing in her stomach. What she really wanted was some hot, strong coffee, but she wouldn't think of that.

Her blood had turned to dark stains on the floor, no longer red. What if someone came here? Shouldn't she leave a message so that anyone who found her bloodstains would know to look for her? At least she should leave the name of—of the man who'd done this to her. She dug out her pizza coupons and pencil, wrote her name and a single-sentence account of the attack on each one, and dumped them under the sink.

Vikki sat on the porch, putting her purse in order and watching the sky turn blue in stages as the sun rose. "Our Father who art in heaven," she said, and stopped. She didn't want to think about fathers. "The Lord is my shepherd," she said. "I shall not want." The sun rose, heavy and too golden-bright to look at behind the electric towers, as she recited the psalm. When she finished, she felt as calm as the morning. She put her purse over her shoulder and walked to the road.

It wasn't much of a road—two pale ruts with grass as high as her knees on all sides. The world looked the same in either direction, but Vikki remembered which side they'd driven up to the house from, and walked that way.

People must come out here, or there wouldn't be a road.

They couldn't come often, or the grass wouldn't be so high.

Vikki had never been up so early. The most she would

be doing at this hour was rolling over, shoving Nikki back onto her own side of the bed, and going back to sleep.

What was happening at home right now?

What had Dad said to Mom? Or had he not said anything? He could be halfway to Mexico by now. There was no reason for him to go back to the house—unless he hadn't been satisfied.

What if Dad had beaten up Nikki—or Mom—or both?

Vikki walked faster, pictures forming in her head, aided by all the cop and horror shows she'd ever seen. Nikki might be dead in a pool of blood right now! If he'd done that, she'd—she'd what?

Get one of Mr. Grant's guns and shoot him dead?

She probably wouldn't be able to shoot straight.

A knife, then. There was a good sharp knife in the kitchen. Vikki planned the attack as she walked, anger urging her feet faster and faster.

"Ow!" Vikki's sandal turned on a rock, her foot twisted, and she tumbled, an unguarded breath jerking loose the pain in her side. She stood up, breathing carefully, till the hurt receded.

"I'm being silly," Vikki told herself. "Odds are he's run off, or gotten temporarily sane again and forgotten what he did. And I wouldn't ever be able to kill anybody, whatever he'd done. And he's got no reason to hurt Mom or Nikki. Get a grip!"

Vikki continued walking at a more sensible pace. Though the sun had risen well above the horizon, when she looked over her shoulder, she seemed to have come a pitiful distance from the house.

If she hadn't been hungry, sore, tired, and miserable, this would've been a pleasant walk—not too hot yet, birds singing, cloudless blue sky, all that stuff. She didn't actually see any wild animals, but once she heard and saw the grass move as a rabbit ran away. She'd never really been out in the country before, but she could see how it could grow on someone.

She looked over her shoulder again at the slowly retreating house. It'd take her all morning to get to the highway.

A ride through the country would've been better. Car, horse, motorcycle—something.

Vikki tried singing to pass the time, but quickly found that it dried her mouth out. Glancing at her watch, she saw that it was almost time for her morning violin practice, so she played air fiddle till her arms tired. Mando had started working on a composition with her, "Duet for Drum and Violin," so she reviewed what she'd heard of it in her head, and soon was planning what to say to him next time they discussed it, working out the technical difficulties. She found herself continuing her side of an unresolved disagreement they'd had night before last, about the future of distinctively Texan musical forms. From there she went on to reviewing the rest of the date: drinking plain Coke in the bar, meeting the musicians, stopping in an out-of-the-way spot on the way home to neck—which reminded her of her father, which made her feel sick and scared again.

Maybe the best thing to do after being picked up on the highway would be to go to the police.

No; it would be less trouble to the person who picked her up to take her to a phone, and once there, Vikki had an obligation to call Mom first. Mom would be frantic by now. She depended on Vikki always being the good girl, always being reliable and doing what she was supposed to do. When Vikki neither came home nor called, Mom would assume the worst. Giving her even one unnecessary minute of suspense would be cruel.

Not that knowing the truth would make Mom any less frantic.

Once, about the time Nikki's dad had left, Vikki had started leaving "God bless Daddy" out of her prayers. Mom had still been hearing her prayers once in a while, and she had insisted on the phrase going back in. "What do I care if God blesses Daddy or not?" Vikki had pouted. "Daddy doesn't like me."

"Don't you talk like that!" Mom had said. "Daddies always love their little girls. You'll understand when you're older."

"Daddies always love their little girls." But what did that mean? She had never understood how Mom could believe that, when both of her husbands had run out on their children. Then Dad came back, and it had seemed that she was right, after all, that daddies did love their children, and would do right by them in the end.

Yesterday he had backed her into a corner trying to get her to kiss him—and he had said, "C'mon, Vikki! I love you!" As if that were simple and obvious and made perfect sense. "That Mexican boy don't love you a bit!"

"It's not the same thing at all," Vikki had said. Something like that. She remembered the sound of his voice, and the smell of his breath; but she couldn't remember whether she had pushed him or just held her hands up between them.

"Not the same!" He'd sounded as mad as Mom did

when she caught Nikki in a lie. "Of course it's not the same! He's nothing to you, and I'm the one that gave you life! You owe me your life, kid—don't you forget that! Why won't you give to me what you give to him?"

"I didn't give him anything!" she'd cried, and he'd hit her.

He couldn't've done that if he'd really loved her, could he?

Vikki had started to shake again, but relief flooded her at the sight of a fork in the road. She changed the subject with herself so fast and so completely that it seemed positively fun to have to choose which way to go.

Shading her eyes with her hands, Vikki peered in both directions. Two roads, one going left, one going right—and which one led to the highway? An attempt to reconstruct in her head the course of yesterday's drive failed absolutely.

Vikki knelt. White rutted lines of earth through grass and weeds; a grasshopper cleaning its face on an old stalk of Queen Anne's lace over here, a dry locust case over there. A shame that car didn't leak oil.

The trouble with the country was it all looked alike. Nothing to tell one direction from another out here but those power lines...Well, she was an idiot, wasn't she? Civilization runs on electricity. So the road that took her closest to those silver towers would take her to civilization.

Vikki walked as briskly as she could toward the power lines, digging in her purse for Chap Stick.

NINE

Nikki Tells the Truth

MOM WENT THROUGH VIKKI'S ADDRESS BOOK, WHICH she found on the vanity. When Nikki put a bowl of cereal in front of her, all Mom did was push it aside. Nikki had a hard time eating, herself. What if Vikki had been shot? Gangs had shot people at the mall before. What if she'd been taken away by a UFO? Or kidnapped by a drug dealer? Or run over by a truck? Or—

Mom started calling relatives, neighbors, friends, people from work, hospitals. With each call her voice got sharper, her queries more urgent, as her possible ways of finding out where Vikki was got fewer and fewer. No one knew anything. No one had seen or talked to her. Everyone made some remark that Mom answered by saying, "I know. It's not like her at all. Something must have happened to her, or she would have called."

Mrs. Lozano was the first person to come over. She took

the phone out of Mom's hands and marched her to the table as if Mom were Nikki's age. "You're not doing any good starving yourself," Mrs. Lozano said. "I'll make you some eggs and toast." The cereal Nikki had fixed sat on the counter, a soggy, unappetizing mess.

"Vikki could be dead in a ditch, and you want me to eat?" wailed Mom.

"Vikki is not dead in a ditch," snapped Mrs. Lozano, banging around in cupboards and the refrigerator. "She wears her seat belt, doesn't she? She never runs with gangs or junkies or that kind, right? So what could happen?"

"Those gangs do drive-by shootings all the time—"

"If she were shot she'd be in the hospital, and they'd've called you by now."

"She could be mugged unconscious and her purse stolen so they wouldn't know who to call."

"Nothing like that on the news this morning. You calm down. Nobody's going to hurt a sweet kid like Vikki." Mrs. Lozano almost ran into Nikki on her way to the stove. "Why don't you go out and play?"

"I don't feel like playing," said Nikki.

"Don't you start! When Vikki shows up safe and sound, you'll be mad you wasted a great morning like this on worrying about her!" Mrs. Lozano steered Nikki outside and shut the screen door. "Look, there's Mr. Grant's kitty. I bet she's waiting for you to come play. Go on."

Fuzzface was stalking a grackle near the crape myrtle, head down, tail tense, obviously not waiting for anyone. Nikki sat on the edge of the porch.

Mando arrived with a new list of people to call and

turned the radio on to a news station. Neighbor ladies came in and out, drinking coffee, saying the same things over and over. Rudy came out back for a while. "My mom says Vikki's run away," he said.

"Your mom's stupid," said Nikki. "She wouldn't do that."

"I bet she did. If you were my sister, I'd run away."

Nikki hit him. He couldn't hit back because she was a girl, so he left.

A couple of times during the morning, the phone rang. Everyone fell quiet, and Mando turned down the radio, while Mom answered. Old Brown Teeth called, then Mr. Grant; and while Mom was wailing questions at him, Andy arrived. He looked around the full kitchen and said, "What is this? Grand Central Station?"

Mom laid down the phone and looked at him blankly.

"What are you doing in your bathrobe still?" asked Andy. "Get ready to go."

"Go?" Mom looked dizzy.

"The picnic," said Andy. "The one we were going on while Vikki took the kid shopping."

"Vikki's gone," said Mom. "I called. I told you."

"Yes," said Andy, "but that shouldn't change our plans. You're all worked up, and all that probably happened is she was out driving with somebody and they didn't stop driving. Didn't you ever do that?"

"Vikki wouldn't run off without calling me!" Mom's voice sounded full of cracks.

Andy put his arm around her. "Every kid does something like this one time—just busts loose. She'll be back this afternoon wondering why you're so strung out.

C'mon, a picnic will take your mind off things." He tried to kiss her.

Mom pushed him away. "She could be dead!"

"Oh, give me a break!" Andy was getting mad now. "Vikki's not as perfect as you think. I bet she did this on purpose. I bet she's got some half-baked plot to get you back together with her dad and this is part of it. She—"

Mom started screaming, "Get out! Get out!" and beating on him with her fists. Mrs. Lozano and a couple of other neighbor ladies rushed to support her, and Mando hustled Andy out again. Nikki curled herself tight around herself, chewing her knee. Mom got a grip on her feelings, taking deep, ragged breaths. "Sorry. Sorry. I didn't mean to do that. Only...Vikki's a *good* girl. He's got no business talking about her like that!"

Mrs. Lozano patted her shoulder and said, "We all know Vikki's not like that. When she shows up, she'll have a good explanation." Her voice sounded kind of fake, as well as soothing, as if Mrs. Lozano were saying the first thing she could think of to calm Mom down, whether or not she believed it.

Fuzzface had vanished. The porch was boring. Nikki thought that if she didn't do something besides be scared she'd throw up or explode. She walked up and down the length of the porch a few times, but couldn't muster the courage to go through all those people to get to her room. Probably if she walked around the house to the front door and tiptoed to her room, nobody would notice her.

Old Brown Teeth was driving up as she rounded the corner. He slammed the car door behind him and hurried up the sidewalk, his face twisted and grim. "Has she turned up yet?" he demanded.

Nikki shook her head.

"I should never have left her." Old Brown Teeth hurried inside. "She said it was all right, said she knew the girl, said she'd call—"

The sound of the door brought people boiling out of the kitchen, blocking the hall. Nikki hung back. She'd have to push past Mrs. Lozano to get to her room now.

Mom ran up to Old Brown Teeth, words spilling out of her like water out of a hose. "Mr. Grant ran that name through his computer that links up to the Department of Public Safety. He says there's three Jennifer Joneses with drivers' licenses, but they don't match the description, and he's called them all, but they claim they don't know anything." She was almost crying, hard to understand. "Isn't there anything—anything else you remember?"

Old Brown Teeth swore. "Maybe it wasn't Jones. Johns? Bones? Doan?...I don't know."

"What did you do?" asked Mando. "Where did you go? And when? We can take her picture around and talk to people."

Nikki spotted one of her coloring books on the coffee table, and tiptoed to get it.

"Let's see...I picked her up here—what?—one o'clock? Twelve-thirty? We went straight out to Windsor Park Mall, shopped all over—"

"Which stores?" asked Mando.

Where had the crayons gone? Nikki poked under newspapers, behind the couch, on top of the TV.

Old Brown Teeth sounded annoyed. "All of 'em, seemed

like! What difference does it make? The place was packed with people shopping for school. Nobody'll remember us. I know we went in at Sears, hit all the shoe stores, all the department stores. When we were about finished we got an Orange Julius and sat down in the food court, and that's where this Jennifer person showed up. Vikki acted like she knew her. Jennifer was meeting some friends for a movie and asked if Vikki wanted to come along."

"What movie was it?"

Old Brown Teeth frowned and studied on the question.

Nikki found the crayons under a seat cushion. The box was all squashed out of shape and wouldn't close right anymore, so the crayons kept sliding out.

"I don't remember," said Old Brown Teeth. "I think it was at the mall, but I don't remember anybody actually saying that."

"We could look in the paper," suggested Mrs. Lozano.

Old Brown Teeth brightened. "It would've been an early show, because Jennifer said they had to hurry. Four-thirty, five o'clock."

"But you were home by then," said Nikki.

Everyone looked at her.

"What are you talking about?" Old Brown Teeth demanded. "It was almost seven when I got home."

"No, it was the middle of the afternoon still," said Nikki, "because it took me forever to get home from your house, and Mom had just got back from work."

"You were never at my house," said Old Brown Teeth. "You went to Mrs. Lozano's, and Vikki and I went straight to the mall and were there all afternoon."

Something went click in Nikki's head. "You're a liar!"

she burst out. "You went out into the country. I don't think you had time to get to the mall, even when I was asleep." She clutched Mom's bathrobe, trying to get the truth out all at once. "They went the wrong way—Vikki said so—and it took so long I fell asleep, so I don't know where they went. But when I woke up she was already gone—"

"Nikki, hush!" Mom roared. "Nobody knows what you're talking about. You said you hung around here yesterday."

"I was lying! I didn't want to stay with Mrs. Lozano while Vikki got to go shopping, so I hid in the back of the car. But they never got to the mall so I never got to jump out and surprise them and I had to get home all by myself on the bus. And then I made up a story—"

"Like you're doing now," interrupted Old Brown Teeth, softly and firmly.

"How could you!" howled Mom, grabbing Nikki and shaking her. "You bad horrible little snot! How could you? How could you? How could you!" Tears streamed down her red face as she started slapping Nikki, who stood and took it, unable to run away or cry or do anything at all, till Mando scooped her up.

Mando hauled her through the press of people, and Nikki started howling, too. Mando took her to the back steps and sat down with his arm around her. When Nikki's sobs turned into hiccups, he said, "You want a Kleenex?"

Nikki nodded, sniffing noisily.

Mando went inside to fetch the box of tissues from the counter. He tried to clean her face for her, but she did it herself. As she blew her nose, he said, "I can see where it's not easy being Vikki's kid sister. I don't even blame you for lying sometimes. But this is the absolute worst time in the world to tell lies."

"I'm not!" sniffed Nikki. "Old Brown Teeth Dave is."

"Why should he? He's Vikki's dad. He wants to find her as much as your mom does."

"So do I! Why would I tell lies?"

"You tell lies all the time. Who says you need a reason?"

Nikki stood up. "I hate you! And I hate Mom, and I triple-hate Old Brown Teeth! I hate everybody in the whole world but Vikki, and she's probably dead! I bet Old Brown Teeth's a cannibal really, and he ate her up!"

"Now, Nikki," said Mando gently.

Nikki kicked him, barely hearing his words through the roaring in her ears. "Just go away and leave me alone!"

So Mando went inside, and she was alone.

TEN

Vikki Has Some Company

VIKKI HAD STOPPED NOTICING ANYTHING BUT THE PAIN in her body, the hunger in her stomach, and the dryness in her mouth. She stumbled and almost fell in the long grass. Catching herself, she saw nothing that might have tripped her, but noticed that she was standing on one sandal that was crooked. One of its straps had broken.

These shoes had been supposed to last Vikki another two or three months, till cold weather came. She took the broken one off and examined it. Maybe she could get it fixed; but she wasn't about to cart it around with her. "I don't know what I did to deserve all this," she muttered, jerking off the other sandal and tossing them both into the grass. She'd never littered before in her life, but what choice did she have?

Vikki pushed her glasses up her sweaty nose and wiped her hair away from her forehead, wishing she had something to tie it back with. Heck, why not wish for a chicken dinner and a car while she was at it? And an anesthetic for the pain in her side—she was beginning to fear she might have broken ribs. And a great big glass of...Coke, water, anything! She realized that her legs were trembling, and for a minute feared she wouldn't be able to make them continue walking. But moving on was the only option she had, and with an effort she did it. Her shadow had grown small beneath her. It must be around noon. After all this walking, why hadn't she made more progress?

Probably, Vikki reasoned, she just wasn't walking very fast. She could hardly expect herself to, the shape she was in. Maybe she should rest during the heat of the day? Any one of the stands of live oaks she was passing would be shady and relatively cool—but if she fell asleep, and anyone came by, she would neither see nor be seen. So she walked and walked and walked, while her shadow swung around behind her and the pain of each step drove out thought.

Her body trickled sweat, but her mouth was dry. The Mexican soldiers that Santa Ana had marched across the desert to the Alamo had chewed chicle resin to keep their mouths moist, Vikki remembered from her history classes. After his capture by General Houston, when Santa Ana went to New York City to await the arrangement of his ransom, he'd taken the chicle with him, and introduced chewing gum to the United States. Her teacher had said it was probably the only useful thing the old villain ever did in his life. She'd see how useful it was, she reflected, digging around in her purse. Something was wrong with her balance; it was actually hard to look for gum and walk at the same time! However, she found the half-used pack of Doublemint, took a stick without stopping, and chewed it till long after the flavor was gone, till her jaws were stiff.

Her head still ached and her shadow bobbed behind and beside her. The shadow of the power lines seemed to grow out gradually to meet her.

The world had a rhythm and a sway that seemed to form into a fragmentary tune in Vikki's head. When she concentrated, she could break it down into the movements of her body, her pulse, and her breathing, with the waving heads of grass adding variety. When she relaxed, all these blended until she could almost hear the sound in her head. The rhythm track was obvious, but somewhere there was a melody, too. She hummed softly, trying to catch it.

The land sloped upward slightly, toward the hills behind the power lines. The sun was too bright and hot. Now that it was mostly behind her, Vikki could see where she was going a little better; but the shimmer of the hot air made everything she saw suspect. She wasn't seeing water mirages as often as she would have on the highway, but she sometimes wasn't sure what she was looking at— waving grass and ruts, or a puddle. The puddles never materialized, and she quickly stopped believing in them.

And the movements in the grass—wind? Animals?

And those dark shapes—did they really move, or were they only distant tree clumps, jerking with the motions of her eyes?

And was a barbed-wire fence blocking her path, or was

that heat shimmers and distance and the blur of sweat in her eyes?

Finally she got close enough to be sure—a barbed-wire fence, a cattle guard, and a gate! The dark shapes were moving, although very slowly. They were cattle! Vikki leaned on the bar of the gate, her heart bounding with unreasonable happiness. If she could milk a cow, that would be food and drink. Her health teacher last year had said that milk was mostly solids. But could she milk a cow if she tried? Could she even get close to one? And what if she ran across a bull?

Vikki focused on the closest animal, lying peacefully, working its jaws, a hundred yards away. As long as it was lying down she had no way to tell whether it was a cow, a bull, or a steer; and even at this distance it looked awfully large, its red sides casting a solid, square shade. It watched her without any sign of interest.

Vikki's stomach growled.

She climbed over the gate. Grass swatted her bare legs as she left the tire tracks. The nearest animal turned its head toward her, jaws moving, brown eyes empty. Vikki walked more slowly, made uneasy by its size and its complete lack of response to her. "So," she said, stopping a few feet away, "what are you? A cow, a bull, or a steer?"

Its ear twitched a mosquito loose, and its tail made a startling *whap* striking its side.

"I don't suppose you'd stand up?" Vikki asked.

The creature twitched its skin.

"Oh, well." More cattle stood by some trees. She'd go see if they were any more cooperative.

Vikki soon found that the grass was laced with paths.

She had to step carefully around the cowpats, but it was still better than wading through grass, which made her legs itch and slowed her down.

The cattle near the trees were less calm-natured than the first one. When they noticed her coming, they scattered before she could even be sure any of them were cows. The next group she approached were all steers, and the next bunch ran away.

By now the sky had turned pink around the edges, and Vikki was so tired, hungry, and thirsty that she wanted to scream, but she didn't have the energy. She stood still and took a deep, calming breath, the way her orchestra teacher had taught her to do when stage fright nearly paralyzed her—but the stab of pain in her side put a stop to that at once.

"Mooo." The sound made her jump, it was so close. A huge, white-faced animal lumbered toward her, and she stepped aside, her heart beating unreasonably fast. It pushed past her, udder swinging. The calf trotting behind said, "Moo!" more quickly and on a higher note than its mother had.

Vikki fell in behind them, following their meandering course as closely as she dared. These were Herefords, beef cattle, but a cow with a calf, even a calf as big as that one, was bound to have milk. She'd stick with these two and see what developed.

A cool breeze walked across her hot face and shoulders.

Vikki told herself that everything would be fine, that God had his eye on her and everything would be all right.

When she saw the muddy pond, she began to believe it.

With a joyful croak, Vikki plunged through the grass, cutting across country to the pond, a stock tank for the cattle. She narrowly avoided stepping into a gopher hole, startled a jackrabbit, and caused all the cattle drinking at or lying around the water to look up disapprovingly.

Vikki dropped to her knees on the tank's muddy rim and tried to drink out of her hands, but the water ran out too quickly. She shoved her face against the water and sucked it down, getting it all over her chin and up her nose, but also, most importantly, down her throat.

When she could drink no more, Vikki rocked back on her heels and for a moment was supremely thankful and happy.

Her legs trembled so badly that she could not hold her position, but had to sink back and sit on the trampled mud.

The cow and calf who had led her there slurped water nearby, and a steer watched her warily.

The power lines were no closer than they had ever been. The road was invisible, as were all the cow paths she had used.

In the west, the sky was as vivid as a spilled box of crayons. In the east, the first stars came out.

"Oh, God," said Vikki, her happiness vanishing as quickly as it had come. "I don't want to spend another night out here!"

"Mooo," said the calf.

ELEVEN

Nikki Blows Bubbles

NIKKI SPENT THE AFTERNOON ALTERNATELY WANDERING the neighborhood and sitting on the back porch. She did not go in, even when the police came, late in the day.

After the police officers left, Old Baldy came back and took charge. He asked short, firm questions, interrupting anyone who didn't give him a short, firm answer. He spread a map on the kitchen table and marked it up, dividing people into teams, telling them what to do and when to do it, and then sent them away, until only Mom, Mrs. Lozano, Old Brown Teeth, and Mando were left.

Mrs. Lozano started making enchiladas. Mom, armed with names and numbers Old Baldy had given her, got back on the phone, less frantically this time. The men sat around the table and talked and talked and talked, until finally Old Baldy stood up and said there was nothing more they could do that night.

"Couldn't we start the search tonight?" asked Mando.

"'Fraid not," said Old Baldy. "It's a shame. The first twenty-four hours are the most important. But by the time we got to the area it'd be dark, and I've still got a few phone calls to make before we can get onto private property. We'll start bright and early tomorrow, don't worry. Meanwhile, we all need to get some sleep."

"Easy for you to say," said Old Brown Teeth. "It's not your little girl out there!"

"This is true," said Old Baldy. "Speaking of little girls, where's the other one? Nikki?"

"Somewhere," said Old Brown Teeth. "She's got her nose all out of joint on account of this fuss over Vikki."

"Poor kid," said Mando.

"I don't feel sorry for a little brat who makes up stories like that to get attention," said Old Brown Teeth.

"I'm sure she feels plenty bad about it by now," said Mando. "She loves Vikki as much as anybody."

"Not as much as me," said Old Brown Teeth.

"G'night," said Old Baldy.

Nikki did not turn or look up when he came onto the back porch. It was not quite dark yet, though the sky beyond Rudy's house was pink and orange. Old Baldy sat on the steps beside her and asked, "Seen Fuzzface lately?"

Nikki shook her head.

Old Baldy took a pack of watermelon bubble gum out of his pocket, took a piece himself, and offered her another. Nikki had not had any lunch, and the smell of enchiladas just beginning to cook was making her aware of how hungry she was. Hoping the gum would help, she took a piece. Old Baldy blew a big round bubble. Nikki tried to blow one, too, and failed.

"There's a trick to bubble gum," said Old Baldy. "It's hard to teach because you can't show people. Chew it just enough to get it soft and stretchy, then kind of mash it up against the front of your teeth in a nice even layer."

Nikki tried it, nearly spitting the gum out on her first attempt. Old Baldy continued to give her pointers, until she managed a single, small bubble, and then another.

"I knew you'd get the hang of it," said Old Baldy.

Nikki had begun to forget to be miserable, but she remembered quickly. "It'd be more fun if I could show Vikki."

"Maybe you can show her tomorrow," said Old Baldy. "The whole neighborhood's going to drive out and search for her in the empty places around the mall, and her picture'll be on TV and in the newspapers."

That didn't make Nikki feel any better. "You're looking where Old Brown Teeth told you to look!"

"He's the only lead we've got so far." Old Baldy blew an enormous, pale bubble, sucked it back into his mouth, and popped it with his teeth. "I'm open to better ones."

Nikki chomped her gum fiercely.

"Do you have a better idea?" asked Old Baldy—not sarcastically, but as if he really thought she might.

"You wouldn't believe me if I told it to you," said Nikki.

"Why wouldn't I?"

"'Cause I'm a big liar and everybody knows it."

"I know you tell lies sometimes to get out of trouble."

Nikki chewed. The gum seemed to be making her hungrier.

"Did you know I used to be a cop?" Old Baldy sounded as if he had just thought of something interesting to tell her. "I got pretty good at knowing when people are lying. Take Dave. He's not telling me everything."

"He's not telling you anything!" said Nikki angrily.

"What makes you think so?"

Nikki hesitated; but if he already thought Old Brown Teeth was lying—if he really could tell lies from truth—maybe he could do something. And if he couldn't, wouldn't, didn't believe her, what would it matter? He probably wouldn't scream at her or hit her. So she started to talk, and he started to listen, jaws working on the gum, till she had said everything. When she stopped, he blew a bubble. Nikki waited, and when he still said nothing, asked, "So? You think I'm lying, don't you?"

"No," said Old Baldy. "Sorry—I should've said. I believe you."

"You do really? How come?"

"What you say works better than what Dave said. I can't find his Jennifer Jones, and it doesn't even sound like a real name. He might as well have said Mary Smith. And he's not sure about what stores they went to, or what movie Vikki wanted to see, or what she bought. All of that makes sense if you're telling the truth and he's lying."

Nikki clapped her hands. "So you're not going to look where he told you to tomorrow?"

Lines appeared on Old Baldy's forehead, all the way up to the top. "Yeah, well, there's problems with that."

"Like what?"

"Like it's not up to me. It's up to your mom, and she believes Dave."

"But...couldn't you make her believe me?"

"How many versions have you given her of yesterday?"

"Um...three."

"Don't bet on it, then."

"It's no fair. Old Brown Teeth tells as many lies as me."

"Yeah, but he's smarter about it, and he's a grown-up. Which is another problem. Why should he lie?"

"To keep out of trouble," said Nikki promptly.

"And why should knowing where Vikki is get him into trouble?" Old Baldy watched her face, waiting.

Nikki looked down, tried to blow a bubble, and failed. She remembered those noises, like screams on TV. "He wouldn't...do anything bad to her, would he? Daddies don't."

"Most moms and dads would rather put themselves through a blender than do anything bad to their kids, but if you were scum of the earth before you had kids, having kids won't turn you into Prince Charming." Baldy frowned into the distance. "I brought in a guy once. His baby wouldn't stop crying, so he held its nose and mouth shut with his hand so it'd be quiet. But every time he let go, it started crying again. So he stopped letting go, and he smothered it. And I asked him how he could do such a horrible thing. And he said I should butt out—it was his kid and he'd train it to be quiet however he wanted. Like it'd never been alive. Like it was just this thing he owned."

Nikki shivered, feeling sick. She knew what dead was like. Fuzzface had brought home a dead squirrel once—a limp, awkward little shape, dragging a tail that had been as alive as it, and now seemed twice as dead. "So you think Old Brown Teeth killed Vikki?" she asked in a small voice.

"I didn't say that!" Old Baldy looked at her again, sounding like he wished he could take something back. "Shoot, I should never have told you that story. That was stupid. It was just an example that some people are bad even to their own kids. No, Vikki'd be a lot harder to kill than a baby."

"But grown-ups get killed sometimes."

"It doesn't do any good to think like that." Old Baldy sounded flustered, which was odd in someone so calm. "What if he got mad at her and locked her up someplace till she said she was sorry? We've got to assume she's okay and waiting for us to rescue her. If we get to thinking she's dead, we'll be too busy feeling bad to do our best for her." He blew an enormous bubble till it popped all over his mouth. "I wish I had a better idea where to start looking. Did Vikki and Dave talk about any specific places that you could hear?"

"Uh...Castroville," said Nikki. "And...she said they were going the wrong way when they got on the highway."

"Which highway?"

"The one right here." Nikki pointed.

Old Baldy asked questions and Nikki answered them. He was good at asking questions in a way that helped her remember more than she'd thought she'd known—the kinds of signs on the highways, the brand of gas station, the time on the car clock. He didn't push when she wasn't sure, just asked another question.

Mrs. Lozano came to the door. "There you are, Nikki," she said. "What're you bothering Mr. Grant for? Supper's ready."

"She's no bother," said Mr. Grant. "She'll be right in."

Mrs. Lozano turned away, and he laid his hand on Nikki's shoulder. "I want you to promise me something."

"What?" asked Nikki nervously.

"Don't ever, ever let yourself be alone with Dave."

Nikki had no desire to be alone with Old Brown Teeth, but something about Old Baldy's voice made the hair on her arms stand up. "How come?"

"Because he knows you're telling the truth. And if we're right, and he hurt Vikki, he's just as likely to hurt you, too, if nobody's around. So promise me, whatever you have to do, no matter how rude or naughty you have to be or how much you get spanked for it, don't let anybody leave you alone with him."

"What if he sneaks up on me?" squeaked Nikki.

"Scream bloody murder and run away; and bite him if he grabs you." Old Baldy smiled. "Don't worry. I'm not letting anything happen to my star witness."

The smile made her believe him. "I promise," she said, crossing her heart.

"Good girl," said Old Baldy.

TWELVE

Vikki Sleeps Out

LYING ON HER BACK, VIKKI COULD SEE TOO MANY STARS.

The grass around the water hole was trampled and crushed, showing where cattle past and present had made themselves comfortable. Vikki tried to make a nest, but the grass itched and poked at her bare skin whatever she did to it. One side was too painful to lie on, and even lying on the other put a strain on the sore place, so she lay staring straight up at the sky, counting stars, trying to find constellations. She had never been good at this, never had much practice or been much interested. She located the dippers, and that was all.

"Well, anyway, that's the North Star the handle is pointing at," Vikki told herself, "so that direction is north." For all the good knowing that would do her!

Vikki had never been so tired in her life, but she couldn't sleep. Comfort was impossible, and her brain, which had been numbly going over the same thoughts all day, would not shut off. Every time she started to drift into what looked like it might be a dream, the growling of her stomach would wake her. When Nikki was smaller, they had pretended that they had tigers in their stomachs, who growled when they wanted to be fed. Vikki's tiger wasn't just growling—it was digging its claws in!

Poor Nikki. Mom would be edgy and frantic by now— the odds that Nikki had made it through the day without doing something wrong, and getting spanked for it, were not good. If only she would keep out of the way and do as she was told, it wouldn't matter what kind of mood Mom was in—but Nikki never could be good, especially when Mom was upset. As sure as Mom was tired or worried or mad at somebody else, Nikki would give her a reason for a spanking. It wasn't always a very good reason, in Vikki's opinion, but of course Mom knew best.

For some reason the thought woke Vikki up even more. Of course Mom knew best. That's what parents were for.

But Dad was a parent.

But that was different.

Was it? Would Mom think so?

How many times had Vikki told Nikki, "She wouldn't've spanked you if you'd done as you were told"?

Dad wouldn't've beaten Vikki if she'd done as he'd told her.

But he'd told her to do something wrong. You couldn't treat your father the way you would a boyfriend. Obedience wasn't the point. Goodness was.

Of course Mom would know that Vikki, her *good* girl, hadn't deserved this.

Of course she would.

"Mooo," said a cow thoughtfully.

Vikki sat up, shivering. The night was suddenly unexpectedly cold. A cow and calf—possibly the ones she had followed here, but possibly not—lay nearby, so close to each other that they made one shadow. Their broad, hairy sides would be warm, rising like a wall against the empty night.

Vikki crawled toward them. "Nice cows," she said, sounding stupid and scared to herself. "Good cows. You don't mind if I join you, do you?" Vikki had no idea what the proper way to speak to cows was, but she remembered that cowboys had used to sing to them in trail-driving days. She took as deep a breath as she could and sang the first cowboy song she thought of.

> "Oh, bury me not on the lone prairie
> Where the coyotes howl, and the wind
> blows free,
> In a shallow grave just six by three—
> Oh, bury me not on the lone prairie."

Not the most cheerful thing she could have come up with, but the cow and her calf let her crawl in between them. She continued to sing as she petted them timidly. When the calf mooed and pushed its head into her hand, she scratched its stubby horns. The mother made no objection to being leaned on. After a while the calf's head sagged, and the cow's deep, even breathing indicated that it was asleep.

Vikki leaned her head back and watched the stars falling up and away from her, into a dream.

THIRTEEN

Nikki Vibrates

ALTHOUGH NOBODY HAD REMEMBERED TO SEND NIKKI to bed till after ten the night before, her head was too full and her bed too empty for her to sleep late in the morning. She dressed as soon as she heard the first car in the driveway. Mom dressed, too, which she had never gotten around to yesterday.

Old Baldy pinned a city map onto the wall above the couch and marked it up with felt pens and colored pins. He put people in groups and gave them instructions as they clutched mugs of coffee. Nobody paid Nikki any mind, and she kept her mouth shut.

After Mom had called in Vikki as a missing person yesterday afternoon, Old Baldy had made some phone calls, and reporters had come by after supper. Vikki's picture had been on the TV news last night, and her disappearance was the second story on the radio news this morning. Rudy's mother brought her morning paper and showed everybody the school picture of Vikki that Mom had given a reporter last night. It had been printed on the bottom half of the front page. Old Baldy pointed to the bottom of the article, where the address and the fact of the search was printed. "We'll get some volunteer searchers out of that," he said.

"Thank goodness for reporters," said Mom. "With all this publicity, somebody's bound to come forward."

"Yeah, good timing," said Old Baldy. "Another week or so, you'd be lucky to get the back pages."

"What do you mean?" asked Mom.

"The last couple weeks of August are the slowest news days of the year," said Old Baldy. "Reporters are desperate. They'll put on anything that looks halfway interesting—zucchini festivals, UFO sightings, whatever. A real news story, even a little one, makes them all shout hallelujah."

"This isn't a little story," objected Old Brown Teeth. "Missing kids are all over the news all the time."

"Only the spectacular ones," said Old Baldy. "Lots of kids disappear every day, and most of them show up on their own within twenty-four hours. The ones kidnapped by their own parents during custody battles don't get much press, either. We wouldn't get much change out of the media if it weren't the silly season."

"That sounds pretty cynical," said Old Brown Teeth.

Old Baldy smiled. "I'm a pretty cynical kind of guy."

Nikki decided that, whatever cynical was, she was going to grow up to be it.

Old Baldy and some of the volunteers had CB radios,

so they set one up on the coffee table and showed Mom how to use it. Old Baldy put Old Brown Teeth in charge of the search. "I got a couple of long shots to work on," he said. "I won't be out there much."

Old Brown Teeth eyed him suspiciously. "What kind of long shots?"

Old Baldy shook his head. "I don't want to get your hopes up. Time enough to explain if they pay off. You go out and search—that's where the useful stuff's going to get done."

Once Old Brown Teeth was gone and Mom was fiddling with the radio, Nikki asked, "What're you doing about him?"

"You had breakfast?" asked Old Baldy.

"Who cares about breakfast?"

"You will, if you don't eat something soon. C'mon." Baldy led her into the kitchen and dug around in the cupboards till he found the cereal, bowls, and spoons. He poured them both big bowls of Cap'n Crunch and set them on the table, beside the stack of posters Rudy's mom had run off at the print shop where she worked. The posters showed Vikki and Old Brown Teeth, from a picture taken not long after he first showed up, and gave her name, address, phone number, description, and last place seen—which of course was wrong, since it was based on Old Brown Teeth's story.

"Know why I got them to pick this picture?" asked Baldy.

Nikki shook her head, dripping milk as she poured it over her cereal.

"I told your mom it showed more of her than the school picture, and that anybody who saw her with Dave and then saw her alone might have their memory jogged if they saw her with Dave again. What I really wanted was a picture of them together. I'm going over to the southwest part of town to take it around the neighborhoods you described, to see if I get any nibbles. If I find someone who saw them, it might give us more clues, and it would sure give us a reason to go look in the right place." He picked a napkin out of the holder and wiped his moustache. "You remembered what kind of gas station that was?"

"Texaco," said Nikki, who had worried about it all night, "or maybe Conoco. Something -co, painted red." She had put too much milk in her bowl. She was making a mess. So was he, though. "Can I go with you? I bet I'd know if I saw it."

Old Baldy shook his head. "I've got to keep on your mom's good side. She's already missing one daughter. She's not going to let anybody run off with her other one."

Nikki stuck her lower lip out. "Mom wouldn't care. She doesn't even know if I'm around."

"Sure she does."

"She doesn't even like me. I bet if I got run over and killed dead she'd tell the driver it was my own fault for being in the street."

"I bet she'd beat him black and blue. Even parents who don't get along with their kids get real upset when someone kills them. I know it's a pain and you want to be out finding Vikki, but right now all you can do is sit tight. Don't worry. As soon as I get the search headed in the right direction, you'll be part of it."

Nothing Nikki said could change his mind, and she watched him go, feeling sullen and left out. She wandered around the house, alternately shooed away from the control center and drawn back to it magnetically. Mom and Mrs. Lozano received calls over the CB and moved pins on the upper right corner of the map. It was pointless, of course, but it was the only thing going on. Nikki examined the lower left part of the map, where all the pins ought to be, but she couldn't make sense of it. Vikki might not even be on this map. It didn't go all the way to Castroville.

"Oh, for heaven's sake," said Mom, shoving her aside. "Can't you stay out of the way?"

"No," said Nikki.

The doorbell rang before Mom slapped her. "Go answer that," said Mom sharply. "It'll be more volunteers."

Nikki stamped her feet on the way to the door. She ought to leave, get on the bus, and go back to Old Brown Teeth's place and break in! Maybe Vikki was tied up there, or maybe there were clues, or—she opened the door and glared at the lady on the porch, who smiled as if she were in a toothpaste commercial.

"Wait, don't tell me!" said the lady, holding her hands up and dropping to Nikki's level. "You're Vikki's little sister, aren't you?" Her big hoop earrings swung and light flashed from the crystals hung inside them. "No one will let you help, even though it's your big sister who's missing, even though you have as much at stake as anybody…" She passed her hands in front of Nikki's face and around her head. "You have a lot of anger here. The vibrations are like standing next to a jackhammer. You…*know*—don't you?" The lady's voice sank to a whisper. "You *know*. And no one believes you!"

"How did you know?" exclaimed Nikki.

The lady smiled like the Virgin Mary picture in Mrs. Lozano's living room. "I know lots of things," she said, holding out her hand. "My name is Angie. I've come to help."

Nikki had never shaken hands before, and did so now nervously. "Uh...Come in," she said. "We've got lots of people looking, but they're all in the wrong place."

"Then I'll help you find the right places," said Angie, walking straight to the living room.

Mom had turned on the TV for the morning news, which showed the searchers arriving at some open space behind the mall. The reporter talked to Old Brown Teeth, who made a speech about how worried everybody was, and begged anyone who knew where Vikki was to speak up. Nikki, safely behind all the grown-ups, stuck her tongue out at him. When the weather came on, Mom turned the sound all the way down and said to Angie, "It's good of you to come, but all the search parties have been out for two hours."

"There's other work I need to do before I join a search party," said Angie.

"Oh?" said Mrs. Lozano.

"Are you a reporter?" asked Mom.

Angie shook her head. "I'm Angela Carerra. I'm—"

"Psychic!" said Mom, her face lighting up. "I read about you! In one of those grocery-store papers. You helped find somebody in Dallas."

"I *tried* to find somebody in Dallas. They wouldn't listen to me till it was too late."

Too late? Nikki felt sick.

"I feel—I'm sure—there's still time for Vikki, but none to waste. Is there anything of hers I could handle?"

"I'll get it!" Nikki ran to the bedroom and got the violin out of the closet. When she returned, Angie was kneeling on the couch looking at the map, Mom beside her, Mrs. Lozano watching them both with a slight frown. Nikki was in such a hurry that she banged her shin on the coffee table. "Ow!"

"Watch it!" snapped Mom. "You'll break it!"

"No harm done," smiled Angie, reaching for the case. All her movements were slow and gentle as she took out the instrument and ran her fingers down the shiny, scratched wood. "Ah," she said. "Vikki loves this very much."

"That might not be the best thing," said Mom anxiously. "It was used when we bought it."

Angie shook her head. "She practiced every day, didn't she? Musical instruments are peculiarly sensitive to vibrations."

"But—"

Angie laid a finger on Mom's lip, and Mom shut up. Angie stroked the body and neck of the violin, plucked the strings, swayed gently with her eyes closed.

"This is garbage," said Mrs. Lozano.

Mom gave her a dirty look.

"Even if she's a real psychic, and she's not—"

"Hush!" hissed Mom. "Give her a chance!"

Angie put the violin back into the case, shut it, and laid it on the coffee table. "Of course, this isn't related to the disappearance," she said, "but the impression of her personality is very strong. I'll be able to find her much more easily now." Opening her purse, she got out a long wire with a loop in the middle. "Now, let's see if I can locate her."

Nikki held her breath and crowded up beside Angie as the psychic faced the map, holding an end of the wire in each hand. Eyes closed, breathing oddly, she moved the wire up and down over the whole of San Antonio, starting in the upper right-hand corner—the northeast. The loop passed over the search area, over the central and southeastern parts of town, over the northwest; and then Angie's body jerked. The wire seemed to drag her hands in a circling motion over the lower left corner of the map.

Nikki squealed happily.

Angie opened her eyes. "She's here," she said. "Somewhere...down here...Maybe a little off the map."

"But...that's clear the opposite end of town from where Dave left her!" protested Mom.

"See," said Mrs. Lozano. "She's a fake."

"But she's not!" Nikki burst out. "That's where Vikki is! Over here somewhere!" She whacked at the map with her fist.

"Stop it!" Mom grabbed Nikki's arm and raised her hand, but Angie dropped a hand onto Nikki's shoulder, and Mom hesitated, turning red. "Sorry. She's such a terrible little liar."

"My mother used to say the same thing about me," said Angie gently. "Your daughter has the most powerful, confused aura I've seen in a long time. Please, let me talk to her."

Mom drew back.

"I don't believe this!" said Mrs. Lozano.

"Then leave," said Angie, not rudely. "The presence of a disbeliever can be very disruptive. Now, Nikki—what makes you so sure I'm right? Something you saw? Something you heard?"

"Both," said Nikki.

"She told a horrible lie yesterday about Vikki's father," said Mom. "You can't trust a thing she says."

"Sometimes, when we see things we don't understand, in ways we don't understand, we try to place it in a more familiar context," said Angie. "It's not deliberate lying, just a mixed-up attempt to make sense of the experience."

"Are you saying...*Nikki*...is psychic?" Mom couldn't have sounded any more surprised if Angie'd suggested that the rug could talk.

"I can't tell yet. Let me talk to her." Angie turned to Nikki and smiled invitingly. "Tell me the truth, Nikki. And don't worry. I will believe you."

Nikki's brain had been working all during this. Of course, she didn't know about Dave and Vikki through being psychic; but wouldn't it be neat if she really were? Mom might listen to her sometimes then! "It was like a dream, but it wasn't," she said. "I heard screaming, like in a movie—only it was Vikki. And there was a white house with trumpet vine all over it, and a car—like Dave's car." She didn't want to set Mom off again and spoil everything. "That's why I said what I did yesterday. The cars were alike."

"And you think this was on the southwest side of town? Why?"

"I just do." Nikki watched Angie's face anxiously.

The psychic's eyelids drooped. "Yes. You are right. A white house...a road through long grass...water somewhere. A sense of...loneliness. And power."

"Power!" Nikki pounced on the word. "There were power lines—those big silver ones!"

Angie turned to Mom triumphantly. "This is marvelous. Nikki and I, together, should be able to find Vikki by tonight!"

FOURTEEN

Vikki Misses Breakfast

VIKKI WATCHED THE SUN COME UP OVER A COW'S BACK. Sunday morning, and she hadn't eaten since Friday before noon. The sound of a calf sucking its mother's udder didn't help any. Even if Vikki had known how to milk a cow, she had nothing to milk into. If only she could take it straight, like the calf—

Well, why couldn't she?

Because it's a disgusting idea, thought Vikki. That cow's udder had been lying against the ground all night!

The water in the pond was dirty, too—and she'd drunk that.

Primitive tribes ate grubs and raw animal guts, and all kinds of gross things.

Vikki moved carefully, both to spare the pain in her side and to keep from startling the cow or any of her neighbors, who so far seemed supremely uninterested in her. She approached the cow, talking in a low, soothing voice. "Hello, Mama Cow. I'm not going to hurt you. Not me. I just want a little drink of milk. Or a big one. Or whatever you'll let me have."

The cow swung her head around, watching this intruder creeping up on her flank. She let Vikki touch her side, and stroke downward; but as soon as Vikki touched the leathery-rubbery udder, the cow stamped her hind foot and let out an ominous *moooo*. Vikki flinched and sat back on her heels, wishing she knew more about animals. Could you even milk a Hereford? They were raised for beef. This cow had probably never been milked in her life, except by her calves.

"S'okay, really," Vikki said coaxingly. "Lots of cows get milked every day, and they don't mind a bit." Didn't they? No, they must get used to it. She reached out again and touched the taut bag.

The cow lowered her head, stamped both hind feet, and *mooooed* again. When Vikki moved her hand down onto a teat, the cow jerked loose from the calf, who mooed a pitiful protest, and kicked at Vikki, who cried out in terror.

Vikki flinched backward and rolled into a ball on the ground, feeling how close the huge hoof had come to striking her. It would have landed in her side if she had been a little slower, right on the pain she already had.

Trembling, Vikki remained curled up as tight as an unborn baby until she heard the cow move away and the calf resume suckling. All right; no milk today.

Instead she crawled to the stock tank and drank till she sloshed, wondering if there were fish in the pond and how she could possibly get them out, gut them, and cook them. You might be able to scale a fish with a nail file, but nail scissors would be hopeless at cutting them open.

Theoretically you could start a fire with dry grass and a mirror, but she'd never seen it done.

Better start walking again.

Tire tracks, cow paths, and barbed-wire fences all blended invisibly into the long grass. All the clumps of trees looked exactly alike. Only the electricity-bearing towers offered any hope of civilization, and they seemed scarcely closer now than they had yesterday. At least they provided a goal.

Vikki picked a cow trail and started walking. The world had a curious rocking motion, which in time she identified as an exaggerated awareness of the movement her body made while walking. The tune she had been starting to hear in her head yesterday was clearer today, the melody line running over and around the weary surface of her brain.

By now Vikki didn't care much what Mom would say about Dad's actions or about what she might have done differently. Faced with a choice between disbelieving her good girl and accepting that a father had done something horrible to a daughter he claimed to love, Mom would just have to sort out what she would believe for herself. Vikki was too tired to be angry, too sore to be scared, and too light-headed to worry. Staying upright and moving was enough effort for one brain and one body, working together at their utmost.

Her side hurt—live with it.

Her vision was blurry—live with it.

Her skin was sunburned red and itchy—live with it.

Her stomach was curled painfully around her backbone—live with it. Live, and keep moving.

FIFTEEN

Nikki's Clue Pays Off

NIKKI RAN OUT TO MEET OLD BALDY. "WE CAN START looking in the right place now!"

Old Baldy raised his eyebrows. "How'd you manage that?"

"Vibrations." Nikki grabbed his hand and dragged him to the door. "This lady came and she said I had an aura and people used to call her a liar, too, and she sees the house and everything!"

The smell of the menudo Mrs. Lozano was cooking pervaded the house. Mom and Angie huddled by the map. Baldy sized up the living room with his eyes, then sat down on the arm of the couch. "Hi, Angie," he said.

Angie smiled. "Why, hi, Scott! How're Karen and Bonnie?"

"Well enough to cash their checks. What brings you here?"

"Y'all know each other?" asked Mom.

"I used to work for the Corpus Christi police when Scott was on the force," said Angie. "When did you come to San Antonio?"

"A while back." Old Baldy took a pack of Doublemint out of his pocket and passed it around. "And you weren't working *for* the department. You just showed up."

"She knows where Vikki is," said Nikki impatiently, pointing to the map. "And she says I know, too!"

"We're changing the search area tomorrow morning," said Mom defiantly. "Angie says the abductor took her clear across town and time might be getting short."

"I won't try to stop you," said Old Baldy, "but that outline on the map looks awfully broad to me."

"It's smaller than the search area on the north side," said Angie, some of the gentleness leaving her voice. "My visions are never precise, and one stretch of empty country looks very like another. If you've got information that would help us restrict the area of the search, why don't you tell us?"

Old Baldy laid his finger on a thin black line on the edge of the map. "We should start with this farm-to-market road here. I got a positive ID and a description of a car from a Conoco attendant. The car—"

"Is a dark-green nineteen-seventy-five Dodge," said Angie. "Yes, Nikki and I worked that out ourselves."

"Couldn't we go tonight?" Nikki tugged at his arm.

"What's with this 'we' stuff, young lady?" asked Mom.

Nikki opened her mouth, but Angie spoke first. "Please, Monica! Her bond with Vikki is so strong—I'm sure she's our best chance."

Mom frowned.

"We can't go tonight, anyway," said Old Baldy. "I talked to all the property owners I could, and they're willing to let us search, but they don't want people traipsing all over at night. If anybody broke a leg or got snakebite they'd be liable. By the time we could organize and get there, it'd be dark."

"But she's been out so long by now!" protested Mom.

"A lot of the owners are going searching their own-selves," said Old Baldy, "and they're a lot more likely to find her in the dark than we are. If we leave here by four tomorrow morning we won't lose any daylight, so make sure you get to bed early." He stood up. "I'm going to feed my cat and get out to the current search site. I'll let Dave know what's going on. Um...Nice seeing you again, Angie."

Angie looked at him intensely. "You ought to let Bonnie know you take an interest," she said.

"Mind your own business. Nikki, have you seen Fuzzface?"

"No," said Nikki, "but I'll help you look."

They went through the kitchen to the backyard, and soon found Fuzzface playing with a grasshopper under the crape myrtle. "I'm glad you found my gas station," said Nikki.

"So'm I," said Old Baldy. "The attendant wasn't real confident in his ID of Dave, but the station was painted red, and there was a dog named Lady lying around, just like you said."

"Angie says Vikki's near water."

"Psychics always say that," said Old Baldy. "And they

never say how much water, or how near. That way they can claim to be right whether the missing person is found lying in a mud puddle, or half a mile from a lake."

Nikki didn't see what this had to do with anything. "It must be neat to be psychic. She knew I knew where Vikki was, right away; and she sees auras. That's this colored light around your body. Mine showed her I knew what was going on and Mom wouldn't listen to me. I bet if she saw Old Brown Teeth's aura, she'd know he was the bad guy."

"I hate to let you down, kiddo," said Old Baldy, "but Angie's about as psychic as my big toe."

"But she knew! Right away she knew I knew about Vikki!"

"It's a trick. Or anyway...It's hard to tell. Sometimes these people really believe what they're doing is all mysterious and spiritual, but I've seen Angie in action, and she never picks up on anything she doesn't have ordinary clues to."

Nikki folded her arms. "She says I'm the best chance to find Vikki, and she's right!"

"I didn't say she was never right." Fuzzface trotted up to him, and Old Baldy bent over to pet her before picking her up. "See, some people are smart in the head, and they notice clues, and think about them, and get the right answer that way. Some people, like Angie, are smart in a different way. They notice things, and they read people, and get the right answer that way. She didn't need any stupid invisible lights to see something was up with you. She knew something about the family from the news, and she talked to you, and she picked up on what was going on. Has she told you one thing yet that you didn't know? Like the number of the highway? Or how far Vikki is from it? Or whether or not she's hurt?"

"She says time's getting short."

"I could've told you that."

"Anyway, she's talked Mom into looking in the right place, so I don't care what you say."

"As long as the search party's moving into the right place, I don't care much, either. I got to grab a bite and then go out to the site. I want to see if I can get any change out of Dave. G'night."

As he turned away, Nikki asked, "Who's Bonnie?"

Old Baldy sighed, rubbing Fuzzface's head. "My daughter. You saw her baby pictures in my apartment."

"Why aren't you interested in her?"

"I am, but I'm a lousy dad, and it's none of your business, anyway." He carried Fuzzface inside.

Nikki felt as if he'd shoved her. Who did he think he was?

And what did she care if he had one daughter or one million? She went inside and ate menudo with Mom, Angie, and Mrs. Lozano—and almost enjoyed herself.

Angie told lots of stories about visions she'd had and cases she'd solved. Mrs. Lozano would sniff and wiggle her face around in disbelieving ways, but Mom drank it all in. She kept looking doubtfully at Nikki. "I don't know," she said. "It doesn't seem to me that Nikki's been seeing visions. She's just naughty and tries to cover up."

"The trouble with disbelieving a child when they tell you the truth," said Angie, "is that they stop paying attention to the difference between truth and falsehood."

103

"Yeah," said Nikki. "Why should I tell the truth when you won't believe me, whatever I say?" She put on the most virtuous, hurt face she could manage.

"Monica, you know this is garbage!" protested Mrs. Lozano. "You'll never get a straight word out of this girl again if you let this go on."

"Oh, yeah?" Nikki forgot to look virtuous and glared at her. "We'll find Vikki tomorrow, and then you'll see!"

"If you're so psychic, tell us what the kidnapper wanted her for," said Mrs. Lozano. "Tell us whether she's hurt or not."

"She's hungry," said Nikki. It seemed like a good guess—what was there to eat, out in the middle of the country? She grubbed in her memory for more clues, putting together what she'd seen for herself and what movies had told her about bad guys. "He wanted to beat her up. She screamed and screamed and screamed." Mom looked upset, so she hurried on. "She's alive, though. She's smart. She...um...she played dead, and he went away. But he wanted to kill her." Suddenly a memory flashed through her brain. "He dropped something, getting into the car."

Angie and Mom both leaned forward. "What did he drop?" asked Mom breathlessly.

Nikki closed her eyes and tried to picture it, a dark shape falling past the door too fast to look at. It wasn't square, and it wasn't round....Well, what did bad guys carry? "A gun," she said, making the picture sharp in her mind, so that she was sure she must have seen it. "He was going to shoot her, but she played dead and he left, and he dropped the gun."

Mom's face turned a funny color, but Angie looked almost happy. "A gun!" she said. "That's great! Guns can be traced."

"Well, if somebody finds a gun, I'll believe this stuff," said Mrs. Lozano. "But nobody will. She's making it up."

"I don't know," said Mom, her eyes on Nikki's face.

"Can I have an ice-cream sandwich for dessert?" asked Nikki, seizing her opportunity, as the phone rang.

SIXTEEN

Vikki Burns Up

THE PAIN OF HUNGER HAD FADED, LEAVING VIKKI WITH the drifting, hot restlessness of a fever. Her skin had turned bright red, and she was chewing her last piece of gum. Compared to yesterday, she saw fewer trees and more cactus. Every now and then, she remembered to check on the power lines. They were always far away.

What was the use? She was more likely to die out here than she was to get home.

Even if she did get home, what then?

She could picture the duplex in her mind—a pile of blackened boards and cinders, firefighters sifting through the wreckage and finding the charred remains of Mom and Nikki—and Mr. Grant and Fuzzface, maybe. Why not? Not knowing why Old Brown Teeth (she used Nikki's name for him without even noticing that she had done so) had attacked her, she had no way of knowing where he would stop.

Or did she? For the first time, Vikki tried to remember what he had said to her as he'd beaten her up. "You'll do as I say, young lady!" And half a dozen other things, an empty muttering in her head. If he had hurt her for disobedience, he had no reason to hurt Nikki and Mom.

He had every reason to lie, of course.

What would he do if she made it back to the highway and hitchhiked to a hospital and called the police from the emergency room? Did he have a story worked out?

And if he did, who would the police believe?

Who would Mom believe?

Though she had thought herself beyond anything but dull endurance, suddenly Vikki was crying again, not breaking stride. The tears twisted her face and made her mouth taste salty. She deserved to be believed, and Old Brown Teeth deserved to go to jail, but what difference did that make? If deserving changed anything, she wouldn't be out here now!

Maybe Mom would say she should've done as her father said.

Maybe the police would think she'd asked for this.

Maybe Nikki would be pleased that her big sister had finally been punished for something.

Nothing was too horrible to happen.

The salt of her tears stung Vikki's sunburned cheeks. The physical discomfort was a welcome distraction from the endless treadmill of thought. Vikki wiped her face, wincing at the pain as skin scraped skin. If only she had some lotion!

She'd always carry lotion from now on—and gum—and a little food—and those moist towelette things. She took off her glasses to wipe her eyes, got salt into a sore where

107

the nosepiece had rubbed, and found new tears starting.

Vikki wished she had dark skin like Mando. He did burn, but it took him forever. He said it was the Indian in him.

The Indians who'd lived in south Texas when the Spanish came must have been sunburned sometimes. What did they do about it?

Wait a minute. She knew that, if she could only remember.

Back when she was Nikki's age, she'd gone to a class at the Witte Museum to do Indian things. She'd made a spear-thrower, a rock painting, and a basket; and she'd pounded some kind of cactus with a rock to make sunburn lotion.

Vikki couldn't remember what kind of cactus it had been, but she only had yucca and prickly pear to choose from here. She was pretty sure it hadn't been prickly pear. She waded toward the nearest clump of yucca, ignoring the rasp of grass blades and seed cases against her legs.

The yucca was a stack of pointed, fleshy cactus leaves, bristling around a woody stem and rising as high as Vikki's head. The leaves themselves were smooth, but their edges were sharp and spiny, and their tips as sharp as pins. Vikki tried to break off a leaf, but there was no smooth space to grasp it by. Sucking a pinprick of blood off her hand, Vikki studied the situation.

She needed a tool.

Sitting down cross-legged, she rooted around in her purse till she found her manicure set. Clippers, nail scissors, file, orange stick. They'd have to do. She scored the base of a leaf with the tips of her nail scissors, then patiently sawed through it with the file.

It took a long time.

Eventually she broke it off, sawing with one hand and weighing down the leaf carefully with the heel of the other. That accomplished, she examined the torn end, which was damp, fibrous, and bright green. Now she should pound it with a rock.

No shortage of those. Vikki pounded green pulp loose from the stringy meat of the plant. Soon she had brand-new aches in her wrists and arms from the pounding. The pulp felt good, cool and soothing, but she had to saw off several leaves to make enough to cover her body. The new smell was fairly nice on its own, but did not mix well with her general body odor.

What would Mando think if he saw me like this? she wondered, watching her hands turn green.

He'd better be too glad to see me to care, she answered herself. Otherwise, he's not worth my time.

Vikki tasted the lotion, but the flavor seemed to dry her mouth out. Maybe she could do something with prickly pear.

She went looking, and soon found one, a collection of pale-green, tear-shaped, bristly pads linked into stems. The ground was booby-trapped with old, blackish pads.

After pulling a couple of spines out of her foot with her tweezers, Vikki spotted another prickly-pear plant near an outcrop of rock. Rock beat thorns to stand on, so she waded through more grass and climbed on, reaching for the plant. This wasn't so bad—the layer of dust on the rock protected her feet from the worst of the stored heat, and she was so hot and sore-footed by now that she bare-ly noticed the difference.

The prickly pear was softer and easier to saw through with her file than the yucca had been, but it had too many spines to grip the leaf and hold it still. She tried picking the thorns out one by one with the tweezers until she had one fleshy lobe as smooth as her own hand, and cut it off.

The skin was tough, but Vikki slit the leaf around the edges and tore the two halves apart, revealing its wet, fibrous insides, which she sucked greedily. The juice was warm, and slightly bitter—but wet, wet, wet! All too soon it was gone, and she had to go through the whole process again.

She harvested all the leaves she could reach from the rock, and after she had slaked her thirst, she still had two left. She tucked them into her purse, checked the power lines, then the sun.

It was late afternoon. The power lines did not look as impossibly far away as they had before. Vikki struck out across country, following the straight line of her shadow, and keeping her eyes on the glittering towers of civiliza-tion.

By sunset, she had reached them—a ruler-straight row of skeletal giants marching along a road of mown grass. Vikki followed the line like a highway until she reached one of the towers, then climbed over a strut and sank down inside its four legs with a sigh. Overhead, electrici-ty hummed, on its way to air conditioners and lightbulbs, TV sets, refrigerators. Vikki pressed her forehead against a hot metal leg and tried to force her brain waves to pass a message into it, to follow miles of cable and wiring and speak for her to Mom—to Mando—to anyone. "Here I am; come get me!" She imagined her voice creating a staticky undertone in Mando's radio, her image flickering behind the Sunday-night shows as Nikki watched TV.

Vikki opened her purse, took out a prickly-pear leaf, and slit it open. As she sucked, she tried to plan, but her mind kept wandering off the point. She didn't want to move, ever again.

If she sat here long enough, would someone come to mow this grass road short again?

Probably, but she'd have to wait too long.

She'd have to follow the power lines—but which direction?

Who knew? Who cared?

Vikki stretched out to spare her side, and went to sleep with the prickly-pear lobe in her hand.

SEVENTEEN

Nikki Joins the Search

THANKS TO THE INTERVIEW THAT ANGIE AND MOM HAD given the TV reporters who called during supper, even more searchers arrived Monday morning than had Sunday. Even Andy came, bearing flowers.

"I'm sorry I said what I did," he told Mom. "I didn't realize how serious it was."

"Well, you should have," said Mom, putting the flowers into the vase Vikki had made when she was Nikki's age. (Nikki had once made a vase, too, but it had been too lopsided to hold flowers and had gathered dust on top of the refrigerator, until the day Nikki broke it.) "But thanks for coming."

A lot of people from Mom's work had come. Mom had given the TV reporters her boss's phone number, and he had said on the TV that anybody who wanted to help in the search could get off today. Mrs. Lozano and Rudy's mother would stay in the living room and monitor the CB radio, and everybody else—including Nikki—was heading out to the country southwest of town.

The sun was not yet up when Old Baldy loaded Nikki into the Jeep between him and Angie, with Mom in the back. "I've got a bad feeling about this," said Old Brown Teeth, leaning on the window. "Chasing after visions, when the first area's not half searched—it don't make sense."

"We're not chasing after visions," said Old Baldy, putting the key in the ignition. "I got a positive ID on a picture. From a man in a Conoco station."

Old Brown Teeth drew in his breath, and his eyes flashed over to Nikki. Nikki watched his face, trying to make her own blank and hard. Old Brown Teeth knew Vikki hadn't been at the Conoco station; he knew the picture Old Baldy had to show around was his own picture as well as Vikki's. He must know he was caught now, that the gas station attendant would be able to back up Nikki's story about where Old Brown Teeth had really been that afternoon.

"Gas stations see hundreds of people every day. It can't be a good ID."

"Why not?" asked Mom. "Vikki's got a memorable face. And it links up with Angie's vision."

"Mine, too," said Nikki, feeling safe beside Old Baldy. "I saw it clear as clear."

There wasn't much Old Brown Teeth could say to that, except to admit that he knew Vikki hadn't been at the Conoco station because by then he'd already hurt her and left her. Life would be so much easier if he did! Nikki glared at him, willing him to say it.

"I hope we don't all regret this," he said, going to his own car, which he had cleaned out to hold searchers.

Nikki's stomach hurt as they pulled onto the highway—as near as she could tell, the same highway at the same place as four days ago. The Jeep was too noisy for conversation, and only growling noises came over the CB—people talking on different parts of the airwaves. Old Baldy passed peppermint gum around. Everyone chewed except Angie, who closed her eyes and did breathing exercises, trying to "catch the vibes." Nikki closed her eyes and tried, too, chewing in rhythm; but it was too hard to keep her eyes closed in the bouncing Jeep. She watched over the dashboard as the sun rose. The city got thinner, then thinner, then stopped being city at all.

As they drove down a two-lane paved road between fields dotted with cows, cactus, and clumps of trees, Nikki started having trouble breathing. That was the overpass right there—in a minute they'd see the Conoco station! Nikki sat up straight. But they passed right under the overpass, and the gas station they saw was an Exxon. Old Baldy turned onto another two-lane paved highway. Nikki slumped in the seat.

Three more overpasses disappointed her before she saw the Conoco station, and then she thought for a minute it wasn't the same one. It looked different from this direction. Then, as they pulled into the paved area next to it, the dog stood up by the rest-room doors, and Nikki cried out, "That's it! That dog!"

Angie's eyes flew open.

"What about the dog?" asked Mom.

"This is the right gas station! I saw the dog." Nikki wiggled around in her seat belt. "I *told* you that."

"You've *told* me a lot of things," said Mom.

Old Baldy opened the Jeep door. "Anybody that wants to be first in line for the rest room better hurry up," he said.

Mom made Nikki use the rest room. When she came out and Mom went in, Old Brown Teeth strolled over to her, smiling. "Hey, Nikki," he said in a friendly way. "What's this psychic business?"

Nikki looked around for Old Baldy. He stood by the air-and-water machine, talking to the boy who'd been so anxious to go into the rest room when Old Brown Teeth was taking so long. "I'm not supposed to discuss it," she said, moving away from him. "It spoils the vibes."

Old Brown Teeth reached a hand toward her. "It ain't fair that detective guy should get all the psychic help! Why don't you come into my car for the search?"

"No," said Nikki, and ran toward Old Baldy and the boy.

Old Brown Teeth, seeing that the two of them were looking in his direction, did not follow.

The name on the boy's shirt was Mike. "I'm pretty sure that's the guy," he was saying as Nikki came up, then shut his mouth quickly.

"S'okay," said Old Baldy. "Nikki here knows all about it. She's the one tipped me where to look."

"There wasn't any little girl with the guy I'm remembering," said Mike.

"I hid in the backseat," said Nikki. "I saw you, and Lady the dog. You wanted to use the rest room, but Old Brown Teeth wouldn't let you in."

"That's right," said Mike. "It must be the same guy, then. Yeah, I guess I'd say it in court."

"Good," said Old Baldy.

Angie and Mando came over, carrying cold drinks. Mando was sweating (but then, they all were) and looking worried. He said to Nikki, "I hear you've been seeing visions."

"She's a very powerful little sensitive, at least where her sister's concerned," said Angie. "When we find that gun, it'll be a tremendous piece of evidence."

"What gun?" asked Old Baldy sharply.

"He dropped it, getting into the car," said Nikki.

"You sure?"

"What is this?" asked Mike. "Visions? I thought—"

Angie smiled her dazzling smile. "I'm Angie Carerra. I came here to see if my gift could be of any help, but it turned out there was already a psychic on the job. Nikki's astonishingly talented."

Nikki knew the look that came over Mike's face. He'd stopped believing what he was hearing. "Look, I've got to get back to the register. I'd like to swear to this guy, but I'm not—I see so many guys, and maybe this wasn't even Friday—I don't know. I'll help y'all any way I can, but—I got to get back to the register." He walked away.

"Thanks a lot, Angie." Old Baldy sighed.

Angie opened her eyes wide. "Why, what's the matter?"

"The matter is, if we get something to take to court and that kid won't talk because you spooked him with your psychic gobbledygook, I'm going to hang you by your thumbs."

"I wish somebody'd tell me what's going on," said

Mando. "Is that the guy you got the positive ID from?"

"Yeah, and now Angie's scared him off." Old Baldy looked down at Nikki. "You sure about the gun?"

Nikki nodded, although her stomach had started hurting. It wasn't Angie who'd scared that boy off, she knew; it was her. He'd decided he was sure when she said she'd been hiding and seen him, but then he found out she also claimed to have had a vision. He'd known she must be lying one time or another, so he couldn't be sure anymore.

"What about shots?" asked Old Baldy. "Did you hear any?"

Nikki shook her head.

"That's good, as far as it goes."

"Wait a minute," said Mando. "You believe in Nikki's visions, but not Angie's?"

"It's too complicated to explain," said Old Baldy. "Get everybody up by my Jeep and let's get this show on the road." As Mando left, Old Baldy looked down at Nikki. "What'd Dave want?"

"Me to be in his car. He didn't think you should have all the psychic help." Nikki folded her arms. "I told him no."

"I should think so," said Angie. "I can't spare your vibes."

Old Baldy picked Nikki up and put her in the Jeep, winking.

Old Baldy spread the map on the hood and took people a carload at a time, making sure they understood where they needed to go and how they needed to act. "There's a lot more ground to cover out here than where you were looking yesterday," he said, over and over again.

"Make a line and walk ten feet apart. Check out every clump of bushes, every tree. You're not just looking for Vikki—you're looking for Vikki's purse, her shoes, her earrings"—his eyes would slide over to Nikki, who had perched herself in the open window of the Jeep and wouldn't move for anybody—"her grave, maybe."

"We'd cover more ground if we walked farther apart," said Old Brown Teeth.

"But we'd be more likely to miss her," said Old Baldy. "This country looks open, but it can fool you. I once walked within ten feet of where we found a kid, and never saw a thing."

Angie circulated around the parking lot, telling everybody about the white house with the trumpet vine, the electric towers, and the gun. Old Baldy's map, which was from the state geological survey and showed trees and rivers and kinds of rock, also showed power lines. There were only two or three in the area, but they were long.

Old Brown Teeth headed for his search area, followed by car after car, till the sun hung whole and yellow in the sky, and only Mom, Baldy, Angie, and Nikki were left. One block of territory was left on the map. Nikki covered it with her hand, feeling fluttery and hopeful again. "It won't take long to do this. I bet we find her this morning."

"I wish," said Old Baldy. "But there's more there than it looks like, and this is only the first map. There's three others she could be on."

"What do we do with Nikki?" asked Mom. "She can't go tramping through a bunch of fields."

"Can too," said Nikki.

"She can stay with me at the rendezvous point," said

Old Baldy, putting his finger on a red X, smudged from all the other times he'd touched it. "Don't worry about her, ma'am."

Mom didn't look worried. "Let's go! If I don't do something to find my girl, I'll break wide open!"

The cars, which had seemed to be so many when crowded onto the street at home and into the Conoco parking lot, looked pitifully few lining both sides of the highway. People had formed their lines and were walking away from the road toward a fence, which the owners had given them permission to climb through. Nikki watched Mom and Angie line up in the assigned sections. They both wore jeans and sneakers and sleeveless shirts, but Angie's earrings glittered in the sun, and she walked with a relaxed swing, while Mom hurried along, jerking her head from side to side. Some people were searching faster than others. In a couple of places, people were holding the strands of barbed wire apart for each other, and Old Brown Teeth was already on the other side of the barbed wire, walking with his head down. The people who lived in the trailer down the road had come out to watch, and the few cars that passed on the highway slowed as they went by.

Nikki kicked the dashboard. "I want to look, too!"

"You'll get your chance," said Old Baldy, "but your Mom's right. You're too small to go running around in the fields. It'd wear you out, and I want you fresh when we get close."

"But it'll be boring."

"May boredom be the worst that ever happens to you." Old Baldy spread the map on the steering wheel and absentmindedly offered her another stick of peppermint gum, which she refused.

"I'm sorry I scared off the guy at the gas station," said Nikki in a small voice. "It was me, not Angie."

"Don't worry about it. He wouldn't've been a very good witness anyway." Old Baldy's forehead wrinkled all the way up to the top of his head as he studied the map. "The more I look at this area, the better I like it. It doesn't show a house, but look—lots of groundwater, which you'd want when you were building, and there's your power lines, right here. Trouble is, at least five other places look just as good on other maps. This is the closest to the station, though, so—yes?"

A shape cut out the light through Old Baldy's window. Nikki jumped, but it was just a man in a cap and T-shirt, leaning against the car door. "You Mr. Grant?" he asked. "I'm Steve Boden. You talked to my boy last night."

"That's right," said Old Baldy. "You're the one letting us walk all over your cow pasture."

"Hey, if it was my kid, I wouldn't've waited long enough to ask permission! We did a little searching for her ourselves this morning—came and drove the cattle into another part of the ranch, get them out of y'all's way—but we didn't find anything. I came to see if I could do anything to help."

"Is there a house somewhere around here?" asked Nikki. "An old house? With trumpet vines?"

Mr. Boden looked past Old Baldy at her, his face wrinkling up in surprise. "Why, how'd you know that, little lady?"

EIGHTEEN

Vikki Rises in the Morning

VIKKI LAY STILL, NOT BECAUSE SHE WAS COMFORTABLE, but because she was sure she'd be even more uncomfortable if she moved.

The humming of the tower had been just loud enough to get into her dreams and make her uneasy. She had woken often with the certainty that someone was sneaking up on her, or was looking for her nearby, in entirely the wrong direction.

The birds signaled morning first, but Vikki didn't move until she actually felt the sun. Then she opened her eyes onto a day like the one before, and the one before that—cloudless, turning blue after a pink-and-green sunrise. She was beginning to feel that she hadn't gotten a new day in all the time she'd been out here.

It should be—what? Tuesday? No, Monday. Friday, Saturday, Sunday, Monday, and still no food, no idea where she was.

Sitting up stiffly (she'd been right about moving) Vikki got the prickly-pear leaf out of her purse and slit it open. Was it her imagination, or was this one not as wet as the ones she'd had yesterday?

She needed to find more prickly pear, or more stock tanks.

And food. There must be something to eat out here.

And she needed—

Stuff all that! Vikki slapped herself sternly, and regretted it. The lotion had all worked in, and her sunburn was as bad as ever. What she needed—the one thing she needed—was the highway.

East and west looked exactly the same, grass and trees and cactus. North and south looked alike, too—grass, trees, cactus, and power lines. Except for the birds, she might've been the only animal alive in the world. She couldn't even see any cows anymore.

The world looked flat and huge, stretching away forever; but she knew from crossing so much of it that it wasn't quite flat. Probably a ridge somewhere rose so gradually that it looked flat till you suddenly looked down at the highway it had been concealing.

What she needed was a mountain. The trees were no good—not very big, and too hard to climb for someone as stiff and damaged as she was. What she needed—oh.

Vikki touched one of the silver struts that made the legs of the tower. The metal was warm, but not yet hot. Eyes and hand followed its diagonal upward till it intersected a horizontal strut, about the level of Vikki's chest. From that point, a neat, regular grid rose ladderlike into the air. The ladder steps were pretty far apart, but not impossibly so.

Not for a normal, healthy person, Vikki thought; but I'm stiff and sore and light-headed. I might fall.

And then?

She might or might not break something. She'd certainly be in pain, but she couldn't fear that much. This was the fourth straight day she'd been in pain; what was a little more or less?

If she broke a leg, she might not be able to travel as far as civilization.

But if she didn't find out which way civilization was, she might starve to death walking in the wrong direction.

Oh, come on. She was less than an hour's drive from town. She couldn't possibly be that far from everywhere in every direction, could she?

Thinking of all the flat, empty country Old Brown Teeth had driven her through, Vikki couldn't convince herself of that.

Climbing power lines wasn't a good idea. She could electrocute herself. That was why, when they had these towers in town, they put barbed wire around the struts, to keep kids from playing on them. She found she wasn't quite sure what circumstances made them dangerous, though. If she didn't touch any actual cable, and went straight up and came straight down—she still might do something stupid without knowing it until it was too late.

That would be true of whatever she did.

She spat on her hands and started to climb, leaving her purse on the ground.

NINETEEN

Nikki Is Right and Wrong

"NEVER MIND HOW SHE KNOWS!" CRIED OLD BALDY. "Where's this house?"

"Up that road over there a piece," said Mr. Boden. "My boy said you asked about houses, but he clean forgot about it. It's been empty so long, it don't hardly seem like a house anymore."

Old Baldy leaned across Nikki and opened the Jeep door. "Let's go check it out."

"She's not there," said Mr. Boden. "I looked for her this morning when I cleared the cows out of those pastures."

"If you didn't take up the floorboards, you didn't look for her. Get in."

Mr. Boden climbed in, and Old Baldy started the Jeep. Several people looked up from their searching, and Dave hurried toward them. Mom and Angie met them at the gate. "Where're you going?" demanded Mom.

Angie rubbed her hands together. "You found the house, didn't you?"

"He knows where there's *a* house," said Old Baldy as Old Brown Teeth arrived.

Mom put her hand on the door handle. "I'm coming, too!"

"And who's going to search your area?"

"She's not in these fields," said Mom. "She's near that house. Haven't you listened to anything Angie's said?"

"Even if she started at the house, she's as likely to be in the field as anywhere by now," said Old Brown Teeth breathlessly. "And there's no reason to think she was ever in any house at all." He glared at Old Baldy.

"What if she's right over there in those trees?" asked Nikki, pointing. "Wouldn't you feel awful?"

But Mom was in no mood to listen. She got into the back with Mr. Boden, and Angie got in front again. Nikki slumped, pouting. Nikki and Old Baldy were the right ones to find Vikki, not anybody else—and certainly not Mom!

"Hey, you're not traipsing off into those fields with the kid, are you?" asked Old Brown Teeth. "What if she wanders off?"

"I won't!" said Nikki.

"You very well might," said Mom. "But if we leave her here, there's no one to look after her."

"I could," said Old Brown Teeth. "If I—"

"No," said Old Baldy, "she's fine where she is. Go back to your own sector—we're losing time." He stepped on the gas and picked up the mike for the CB radio. As he let the other searchers know what was going on (two or three of them had CBs in their cars), Nikki looked over her shoulder and saw Old Brown Teeth staring after them with his fists clenched.

Mrs. Lozano came on the CB to tell them how silly they were being. In the backseat, Mom explained Angie's visions to Mr. Boden, not mentioning Nikki even once. Angie did breathing exercises and concentrated.

The road through the fields was just two ruts in the long grass. Nikki reminded herself that all long grass looks alike, and chewed her fingernails. A couple of times Mr. Boden told Old Baldy to change to another set of ruts when others turned off the first one.

Mom laughed nervously. "This reminds me of high school. You know, driving out into the country forever and ever, looking for a place to park?"

"There's all the parking space in the world out here," objected Nikki, "and no place to shop."

"Not that kind of parking," said Mom. "You'll know all about it when you're bigger."

Nikki remembered Vikki talking about parking once or twice. It was something boyfriends and girlfriends did, to be all alone for kissing and stuff. Boring—but it was funny to think of Mom being a teenager and doing that sort of thing.

Suddenly she got a mental picture of Mom and Old Brown Teeth driving way out in the country to kiss on each other. Gross!

A distant flash of silver distracted her from these unwelcome thoughts. "Look! Power lines!" she said, pointing.

"I see 'em," said Old Baldy. "They're a good sign, but

they don't prove anything." He sounded a little breathless, though.

Nikki's stomach hurt again. When the house came into sight she was sure, then unsure, then suddenly, blindingly, absolutely sure. "That's it! That's it!" she screamed, bouncing up and down on the seat.

Mom reach over the seat and slapped her head. "Shut up! Angie, is this—?"

Angie smiled dreamily as they pulled up where Old Brown Teeth's car had been four days ago. "Yes," she said. "Vikki's been here. I feel the vibrations all through me."

"I just told you that!" Nikki snapped at Mom. "Why do you keep asking her?"

Old Baldy opened the door. "Let's not argue about who believes what, okay? We need to search this whole place—inside, outside, underneath, all around." He got out, and swung Nikki down the long step to the ground.

"The gun!" squealed Nikki. "It should be right around here! He dropped it when he got into the car!" She started hunting through the grass on her hands and knees.

"You know, there's something familiar about this place," said Mom.

Angie answered, "Vikki's been through some very powerful emotions here. Possibly you're picking that up."

"No. No, it's—I know. When Dave and I were in high school, we used to drive out to a place just like this."

"It might even've been the same place," said Mr. Boden. "We get kids out here sometimes. Somebody keeps stealing the padlock off the gate, and we can't keep them out."

Nikki's fingers found something hard and oblong in the grass, though it was still hidden from her eyes. She squealed. "I found it! The gun!" She held it up—but it wasn't a gun.

"That's a Buck knife," said Mom scornfully. "So much for your big psychic abilities."

But...she'd remembered...hadn't she? "I must've made a mistake," Nikki said in a small voice.

"So what else is new? Put it down and stand up. You're getting all dirty."

"Hang on." Old Baldy crouched next to Nikki and held out his hand. When Nikki gave the knife to him, he unfolded it, his jaws working intently on his wad of gum as the blade at first refused to open. When it did come loose, its shiny metal was stained and dull. "There's blood on this."

Nikki's body shook with the force of her heartbeat.

Angie reached for the knife.

Old Baldy held it away from her. "This is evidence. It's bad enough that Nikki and I've already got our prints on it. Get that black box out of the back of the Jeep, if you want to be useful."

"If I could get vibes off it—" began Angie.

"Forget the vibes! Just bring me the box!"

Angie pulled back, frowned at him reproachfully, and went to the Jeep. When she brought Old Baldy the box he got out a paper bag, in which he sealed the knife, then wrote out a label and stuck it on. As he did this he kept talking. "Has anybody seen Dave use that Buck knife of his the last few days?"

"Dave? But—" Mom's face changed color.

"Yes, Dave! He's got a black Buck knife; he's the last person who'll admit to having seen her. This is a natural question!" Old Baldy sounded really angry for the first time since Nikki'd met him.

"But...he's her daddy," protested Mom.

"So?" Old Baldy closed his box with a snap.

"A lot of people have Buck knives," said Mr. Boden. "We don't even know for sure yet that your girl was here."

"That's true," said Old Baldy. "Anyway, I'm a lot less interested in finding who took Vikki than I am in finding her. I'll call back to the main searchers, see what's going on. Y'all spread out and go over every inch of this house. Every inch!"

Nikki crawled through the grass, but she found no more knives and no further trace of Vikki. While Old Baldy was on the CB, the grown-ups, led by Mr. Boden, went to the house, Mom walking slowly. They hadn't been inside long when Nikki heard a scream.

It sounded so much like the sounds she'd heard four days ago that Nikki almost swallowed her tongue. She ran into the building, taking the two porch steps in one leap. No one was in the front room, but in back, Angie knelt beside some blotches on the floor, and Mom crouched crying over a scattering of paper by a metal sink.

"Don't know how I missed all this," Mr. Boden said. "Too dark, I guess. I was looking for—you know—her."

"What is it?" demanded Nikki.

Angie shushed her. "Bloodstains, and a note. See if you can pick up anything."

Nikki shoved past her and hung over Mom's shoulder. She was holding a crumpled Pizza Hut coupon. In the white space between the picture and the price, Vikki's handwriting said, in pencil, "My dad brought me here, and beat me up. Vikki Baum."

"But where's *she*?" demanded Nikki.

Mr. Boden looked helpless.

Mom cried.

Nikki ran out of the house again, shouting, "Baldy! Mr. Grant! Come quick!"

TWENTY

Vikki Makes It to the Top

BAREFOOT AND BARE-HANDED ON METAL, VIKKI climbed until her head was even with the last strut below the actual electric cables. The distance from the ground seemed a mile or two at least, but she wasn't frightened. She didn't have the energy to be.

The light in the east hurt to look at. Shading her eyes, Vikki made out more fields, more fences, and a depressingly distant, empty paved road. North: more of the same and a line of trees—a creek, maybe?—and a house where cows grazed in the yard. Hope, or another empty one? South: highway at last! Only a two-lane country road, but it still meant civilization!

Tiny and toylike, cars had parked along both sides down the road from a trailer, a Conoco station with a tall sign, and a distant overpass. The power line cut diagonally toward the road, crossing it at a depressing distance from the gas station. Well, she'd walked this far. If she had to walk a little farther once she reached the highway, she'd just do it.

What on earth were all those cars doing there, crowding that one section of a little farm-to-market road?

Squinting in puzzlement at the cars, Vikki noticed an oddly uniform movement in the long grass. Once alerted, she could make out the forms of people, working their way in wavy but fairly evenly spaced lines into the field away from the road. Vikki clutched the strut above her head as a wave of dizziness struck her and passed on.

Were they—could they be—looking for her?

No, of course not. Not unless Old Brown Teeth had come to his senses and told them where he'd left her, and in that case they'd be by the house, not the highway. They must be doing something else.

Vikki looked back the way she'd come. A lone vehicle — a funny shape for a car; a Jeep or something—jolted along some invisible road. As she watched, it pulled up in front of the empty house and spilled out two people on the side nearest her. The Jeep's high sides hid anyone emerging from the driver's side.

Mr. Grant had a black Jeep. But this couldn't be—

Vikki found that she was shaking. Who cared who they were! She had to get their attention! Waving her arms and shouting would do no good at this distance. She needed a signal, some way to send an SOS, like Nikki in that castaway game.

Ignoring the weakness in her arms and legs, Vikki began the long climb down.

TWENTY-ONE

Nikki Drops Behind

NIKKI BARRELED INTO OLD BALDY ON THE PORCH. "Bloodstains!" she shouted. "And a note! Vikki left a note!"

"Did it say anything about going anywhere?" Old Baldy grabbed her hand and hustled inside with her.

"No," answered Nikki. "It just said Old Brown Teeth beat her up. Mom's crying."

"Vikki may still be around. Maybe she found a hiding place, and...fainted or something." In the kitchen he strode past Angie, who was stroking a bloodstain and humming, and ignored Mom, who was still crying. "Where is there to hide around here?" he asked Mr. Boden.

"Crawl space under the house, and a couple of closets," said Mr. Boden. "This note—it says her daddy beat her up."

"I know," said Old Baldy. "Nikki here's a witness. Plus

the guy I was just on the CB with says Dave made an excuse and drove off right after we went through the gate. I'll call the searchers, and you and Nikki and I can do the house. I don't think Monica's going to be good for much."

"What about Angie?" asked Nikki.

"Not in the house, nor under it," said Angie in a low, intense voice. "Open air...sky...and bright, bright—"

"Yeah, yeah, fine," said Old Baldy. "She'll try for something more specific, and the rest of us mere mortals'll search the house."

Nikki looked in all the closets and under the porch. Mr. Boden crawled under the house. Mom calmed down enough to gather up the rest of the Pizza Hut coupons and found a contact lens under the sink, dried-up and hard. Angie tried to get vibes from it, but all she saw was an image of Old Brown Teeth beating Vikki up, and the contact coming out when her head hit the sink.

"She's not here," Angie said after walking through the house with her arms outspread. "She tried to follow the road out, but she missed her way. She's lost."

"Heck, I could've told you that," snorted Old Baldy.

He had been on his CB, reorganizing the search to cover the area between the house and the highway without losing any time.

Nikki sat on the porch steps when she ran out of places to look, staring at the glittering power lines. Vikki was out there somewhere, and Nikki had nothing left to do. This was as far as her knowledge could bring them, and it wasn't far enough.

Mom, Mr. Boden, and Old Baldy clustered around the

map, once more spread on the Jeep's hood. Angie sat with Nikki.

"What did Scott mean when he said you were a witness?" she asked.

"I tried to tag along with Vikki to the mall, and I hid in the backseat," said Nikki. "And he brought her here. But I was asleep and didn't see much, didn't even figure out what was going on till she never came home. And then I couldn't get anybody to believe me."

Angie sighed. "And here I thought I had a major psychic discovery! Your mom was right about your lying wasn't she?"

All the admiration Nikki had felt for her dried up. "Mom made me lie 'cause she wouldn't believe me when I told the truth!"

"Maybe you made her disbelieve you by telling so many lies before," said Angie, sounding like any old ordinary grown-up.

"Who cares?" grumbled Nikki. She didn't want to try to explain about how tired she got of Mom hitting her, how none of her efforts to be good ever seemed to work, how the lies were the only thing she could think of that sometimes kept her from being punished. If Angie were a real psychic, she'd know all that, wouldn't she? Angie was a liar, too, only she didn't know it! Nikki hunched up around herself as the first of the searchers' cars drove up.

Angie rose to greet Mando and his father and brother as they got out, but Nikki stayed put, watching sunlight flash-flash-flash, hypnotically, off one of the power towers.

TWENTY-TWO

Vikki Signals

NOW THAT RESCUE WAS IN SIGHT, ALL THE PAINS AND discomforts of the last four days gathered for a last assault upon Vikki. She was so tired and sore that she let go of the tower and dropped the last five feet or so, landing too hard on her injured leg and falling as it folded under her. Her glasses flew off, a stab of fresh new pain shot through her side when she hit the ground, and for a moment the bright world was black to her. She sat and gasped.

No time for this! They might go away!

Vikki groped for her purse and dumped its contents onto the ground, pawing through them as her sight cleared to normal-fuzzy. She found her glasses by feel, and then the mirror. She needed both hands, and had no pockets, so she took the mirror between her teeth, and started to climb.

And climb, and climb. It hadn't been this hard last time—or maybe hope had been dead and she hadn't cared! Vikki was panting and trembling when she got to the top. Was the tower swaying in the wind, or was it just dizziness? Either way she couldn't fall off now! She sat on one strut with her arm linked around another, took her mirror out of her mouth, and began to signal, experimenting to catch the rays of a sun that was mostly behind her. Short, short, short; long, long, long; short, short, short. Pause. Short, short, short; long, long, long; short, short, short.

Little stick figures clustered around the hood of the Jeep; two more sat on the house's porch. More cars came through the fields now, in a long line. At regular intervals, the rearmost car would drop out and unload people, who started moving off crossways to the road, some toward Vikki, some away.

"Oh, look up, somebody!" Vikki moaned, resting her wrist on the burning metal of the strut. Short, short, short; long, long, long; short, short, short. "Somebody, please, look up!"

TWENTY-THREE

Nikki Receives

WHY, NIKKI WONDERED, DID ONLY ONE TOWER FLASH like that?

The grown-ups bunched around the map, arguing about which directions needed to be searched first. A hummingbird darted in and out of the orange flowers on the trumpet vine. Nikki wondered where its nest was and if it had babies. Hummingbird babies would be so tiny she couldn't even imagine them. Nobody'd notice if she went nest hunting. She could do anything in the world she could think of, right now, and nobody would try to stop her, because nobody ever looked in her direction.

Nikki leaned back on her hands. The flashes off the tower had a pattern, if you looked long enough. She counted. Three, short pause; three, short pause; three, long pause. Begin again. The flashes weren't all alike, either. The first and third sets flickered by, all crowded together, while the second set took its time and had longer flashes. It reminded Nikki of something. Short, short, short, she counted. Long, long, long; short, short, short. Just like—

Nikki sat up straight, staring at the distant tower. The long pause seemed horribly long this time; but then she saw the flicker begin again. It was just like that signal Vikki had shown her how to do with the mirror in the desert-island game!

"SOS!" shouted Nikki, leaping to her feet.

The grown-ups turned startled faces toward her. "Nikki, hush!" said Mom.

"SOS!" Nikki was choking too much to say anything else, so she pointed at the tower, lining her finger up exactly on the flashes, and started to stamp her feet, chanting in rhythm, "SOS! SOS! SOS!"

"Nikki, shut up and sit down!" yelled Mom. "We don't have time for your foolishness!"

"Hold on," said Old Baldy. He looked toward the east. "I don't see anything. "What're you pointing at?"

"SOS!" howled Nikki. "Right there!" She jabbed her finger.

"Nikki, I'm warning you—," began Mom, but Old Baldy interrupted.

"Oh, for crying out loud! When are you going to start listening to this kid?" He hurried to the porch and stood beside Nikki. "Calm down and tell me what you see."

"SOS!" Nikki kept stamping her feet and pointing as straight as she could. "Don't you see it? That tower's flashing like Vikki showed me. SOS! It means 'Save our skins'!" She was almost crying. "It's right there! Why don't you see it?"

139

Mando and Mr. Boden came up onto the porch, too, all shading their eyes and trying to follow Nikki's finger. Angie leaned over the hood of the Jeep, peering eastward. "Yes!" she yelped. "In the northwest part of the horizon! One tower has a little flashing white light on top!"

Old Baldy growled impatiently. "I still don't—yes, I do! S, O, S." Suddenly he bent over, scooped Nikki up, and half tossed her into the air. "Three cheers for Nikki! She did it again!" He set her down hastily and joggled Mr. Boden's elbow. "You drive. It's your pasture we're tearing up."

Everyone piled into the two cars, Nikki bouncing between Old Baldy and Mr. Boden in the front of the Jeep. First they drove on one of the sets of ruts, but then Mr. Boden started to cut across country, and Nikki's teeth knocked together as they bumped over the pasture. When they got to a fence, Old Baldy jumped out and threw open the gate, scrambling back in again without taking his eyes off that wonderful flashing light.

TWENTY-FOUR

Vikki Comes Down for Good

AT FIRST, VIKKI DIDN'T BELIEVE THAT THE JEEP AND the second car were driving toward her on purpose.

As they came closer a bubble of hope swelled in her, till she started to laugh and cry and sway on the strut. The wind stung her sunburn, making her eyes water, and her wrist ached from the steady motion of the mirror.

Could she stop now? Oh, please, could she stop? No— one tower looked too much like all the other towers. She didn't know whether she herself would be visible, or at what distance. If she stopped signaling, they might think they had imagined it, might not find her after all. She couldn't bear to be lost again. She'd lie down and die.

Vikki forced her hand to keep moving. The ache spread up her wrist to the muscles of her forearm. The narrow strut cut into the backs of her legs. She lost track of where she was in the sequence of long and short, and just flashed and flashed and flashed, till the Jeep pulled up beneath her and the doors flew open. With a sob of relief, she dropped the mirror.

Mr. Grant, Nikki, Mom, and some strangers tumbled out of the Jeep before the little circle of glass hit the ground. Nikki and Mom led the rush, waving their arms and shouting her name. Mando's family got out of the second car. Vikki couldn't hear what anyone was shouting through the ringing in her ears, but she grinned, waved, and shouted back, "I'm fine! I'm coming down!"

"Vikki!" Mom shrieked. "You'll break your neck!"

Nikki pulled herself onto the first strut like a monkey, but Mr. Grant caught her before she could climb any higher.

One strut at a time, Vikki made her way down to the next-to-the-last rung, where she let go, falling into all the willing hands waiting to receive her. She started hugging Mom and Nikki before Mr. Grant and Mando even set her on her feet. "You're all right!" she mumbled, around tears and laughter and the swollen stiffness of her tongue. "I was so afraid he'd hurt you, too!"

"You don't have to be scared of him ever anymore," said Nikki, hugging Vikki's wounded leg so tightly that Vikki felt sick with pain—but she didn't cry out. "Old Baldy'll catch him!"

Then everyone was hugging her all at once. Mando hung back, as if—as if what? She didn't care; she kissed him. And the world was a blur of pain and happiness.

TWENTY-FIVE

Nikki and Vikki

FOR THE REST OF MONDAY, THEY COULDN'T GET AWAY from reporters, and Vikki had to stay in the hospital overnight for observation.

On Tuesday, she came home. Vikki would be fine, the doctor said, once the infection in her leg was cleaned out, and the cracked rib healed, and the sunburn faded, and she got enough food and drink inside of her. Mom stayed home from work again, and the house continued to be full—more reporters, all the neighbors, people from Vikki's school and Mom's work. Vikki, stretched on the couch, was sweet and polite to everyone. When Mando came over, it was Nikki's job to keep people away while they talked in low voices, with their heads close together. Andy brought pizza, and Mrs. Lozano took a whole carload of people to her church to say thank you to God for letting Vikki come out so well.

On Wednesday, Mom overslept and ran around like a chicken with her head cut off. She left Vikki's breakfast half-ready on a tray and ran to the bathroom for something, so Nikki poured the rest of the juice and took the tray to the bedroom. The bedroom door was closed, so she balanced the tray on one knee while she turned the knob; but the tray didn't balance. The door swung open and the food landed on the floor as Mom walked out of the bathroom.

"Dang it, Nikki!" shouted Mom, raising her hand.

Nikki ducked her head and glared at the mess.

"Mom!" Vikki's voice came out of the bedroom, unexpectedly loudly. "Don't hit her!"

Mom turned her head. "What?"

"Don't hit her," repeated Vikki, putting her hand on the lump that still deformed her forehead. "It hurts to be hit. I know."

"But...Look at the mess she made!"

"She didn't do it on purpose. You were trying to help—weren't you, Nikki?"

Nikki nodded, holding her breath.

"Well...all right," said Mom, lowering her hand. "But she'll have to clean it up. I'll be late to work as it is, making you a second breakfast."

"I can fix my own breakfast," said Vikki. "It's okay. Really. If I don't get up, my leg'll get stiff on me. Go get ready for work. I'll be fine."

So Nikki cleaned up, Mom went to work, and Nikki and Vikki ate cereal together. When Vikki settled on the couch to practice her violin—a hesitant, new tune she'd never played before—Nikki took Old Baldy's key and went next door to feed Fuzzface, as she had promised to do.

Fuzzface went crazy when she saw Nikki, demanding petting, then complaining about the food, making scolding noises as she gobbled it down. As Nikki watched, somebody knocked on the door.

Old Baldy had told her, firmly, to only go into the kitchen. But he couldn't blame her for answering the door, could he? Nikki skipped down the hall, resisting the temptation to check the room with the train as she went past (she was pretty sure he'd locked it) and opened the door without unchaining it.

On the porch, a girl about Vikki's age seemed surprised. "Hi," she said. "I'm looking for Scott Grant."

"He's out catching a bad guy," said Nikki. "Who're you?"

"Bonnie Grant. Who're you?"

"Nikki." She took the chain off and opened the door for a better look. "You're Old Baldy's daughter, aren't you?"

"I'm...Mr. Grant's daughter." Bonnie seemed unsure what to do next. "Is he bald?"

"Except around the edges," said Nikki. "He's got a moustache, though." Now what? She wasn't supposed to let anybody into Mr. Grant's half of the house. Nikki went out onto the porch. "Hey, Vikki!" she yelled over the music. "Old Baldy's kid is here! Take care of her while I lock his place back up, okay?"

Having seen Bonnie safely inside, Nikki returned to Old Baldy's kitchen. Fuzzface was trying to open the screen door, so Nikki let her out, locked up, and went home.

Vikki had set her violin aside, and Bonnie sat in the armchair. "This is so weird," said Bonnie. "We're sitting here, and my dad is out hunting your dad."

"He took a gun," said Nikki helpfully, sitting next to Vikki. "But he won't shoot Old Brown Teeth unless he has to. I hope he has to."

"Old Brown Teeth?" repeated Bonnie.

Vikki laughed. "Nikki's always called him that, and I'm starting to. It suits him better than 'Dad.'"

"It must've been so horrible for you. Your own father—"

"Of course, it was bad. But—I don't know—everybody seems disappointed that I'm not a basket case about it. My boyfriend thought I'd be afraid of men for the rest of my life, and the doctors kept warning me about all sorts of symptoms I'm supposed to have, but"—she shrugged— "apart from a few nightmares, all I feel is happy to be home. Maybe I'm traumatized, and lying to myself about it, and it'll set in later."

"I'd think something like that would divide your life in two," said Bonnie. "Change the way everything looked, somehow."

"Some things look different," said Vikki, slipping her arm around Nikki. "By the way, I don't know which version you read in the papers, but Nikki here's responsible for finding me."

"It was all mixed up in the Corpus Christi papers," said Bonnie. "Some of the stories sounded like Angie Carerra tracked you down psychically, and some of them said Nikki was a witness and led my dad straight to the spot."

"That's the right story," said Nikki, "but Mom still doesn't believe it! She won't even listen to Old Baldy."

Vikki hugged her tighter. "Well, I believe you! And even

Mom knows it was you that first saw my SOS." She looked at Bonnie again. "Did you come down here because you saw your dad's name in the paper?"

"No. Angie called me."

Nikki, at the sound of a familiar engine, wiggled free of Vikki and went to the window.

"Angie? What, is she an old friend of your family?"

"Sort of. She knew my dad back when he was still with the police, and Mom and I met her once or twice. He didn't like her much. I didn't think she liked him. But she called, and said he was sober now, and didn't I think this was a good time to see him? And I read all the newspaper stories, and I thought about it, and...here I am."

"And here he is," announced Nikki. "I'll go get him." She ran to the door and yelled out as the Jeep parked in the driveway, "Hey, did you get him? Did you shoot him?"

"Better'n that!" Old Baldy got out of the Jeep with a folder under his arm and came up onto the porch.

"What's better'n shooting him?" asked Nikki as they went in.

"Getting a signed confession," said Old Baldy, walking into the living room. He stopped, looked blank for about two seconds, and said, "Bonnie?"

"Hi, Daddy," said Bonnie shyly.

"Uh...Where'd you come from?"

"I drove up to see my dad. Anything wrong with that?"

"Well...depends on the dad, doesn't it?" The top of Old Baldy's head had turned red. "Not that I'm not glad to see you. But—" He looked at Vikki. "There's dads and there's dads."

"But you're nothing like Old Brown Teeth," said Vikki.

147

"Angie says you've been sober a long time," added Bonnie.

"Yeah...well...I knew a guy who was sober for twenty years, and then one day he took some NyQuil for a cold. The next time anybody saw him he was dead in a motel room with a bottle of Thunderbird in his hand. You think I would've stayed away so long if I thought I was trust-worthy?"

"You can talk about all that *later*," Nikki said, tugging at the file folder. "What about Old Brown Teeth?"

"Right." Old Baldy sat down on the hassock and fished a box of Chiclets out of his shirt pocket, passing it around before tossing the remainder of the box's contents into his mouth and talking around the crunchy chewing. "I didn't have too awful much trouble finding him. He's not a bright man. So I caught up to him in this motel outside of Houston last night, and took him for coffee, and pretty soon he'd decided I was his best friend. He wrote every-thing out all nice and pretty on a legal pad and let me drive him to the nearest police station for booking." He opened the folder and passed some photocopies to Vikki. "The cops have the originals, but you can't have too many copies of something like this."

"How'd you do this?" asked Vikki, looking over the gray pages. Nikki tried to read over her shoulder, but it was all in blurry cursive, and she couldn't make it out.

"Oh, getting folks to talk is easy," said Old Baldy, "if you don't mind washing your mouth out with soap after-ward. I let on like I was on his side, like you were a terrible flirt and full of yourself and probably had it com-ing, and pretty soon he was spilling his guts. So then I bring out my legal pad, and I'm talking about how important it is to have his side of the story, how you're going to flutter your eyes at the jury and they'll believe anything you say. Pretty soon he's asking me how to spell *abandoned* and when will he get his Buck knife back."

Nikki frowned at him thoughtfully. "You lied to him."

"Yeah, I guess I did."

"So how come it's okay when you do it?"

"Nikki!" said Vikki reproachfully.

"S'all right," said Old Baldy. "It's a fair question, and I don't know the answer. All I know is, I've got a talent for that kind of lie, and it's good for catching the bad guys."

Nikki thought about that, while Old Baldy went into details about how he'd tracked Old Brown Teeth down. Bonnie talked about her mother, and asked Vikki questions about being lost.

After a while Old Baldy and Bonnie went next door. They seemed to be getting along okay. Old Brown Teeth and Vikki had gotten along all summer, Nikki remembered. "Bonnie's dad isn't a bit like yours," she said to Vikki.

"No," said Vikki. "Not a bit."

"What does *sober* mean?"

"It means he used to drink too much beer and stuff, and make everybody around him miserable, but he doesn't anymore."

"Oh." Nikki thought about that. "Old Baldy used to be bad, but he's good now. Right?"

"Well...He used to act bad, and now he acts good." Vikki put her feet up on the couch.

"Even if he does tell lies sometimes."

"Nikki, honey, what's eating you?"

"Maybe by the time I'm grown up, I'll be good, too."

"You're good right now," said Vikki. "Whatever Mom says, you're the best little sister I could possibly have. And you've proved it by sitting around with me for two days! Is there something you'd like to do? I can't go swimming, but we could play something."

Nikki perked up. "Could you play jacks?"

"You bet," said Vikki. "Bring 'em on!"

Nikki jumped up and ran to the bedroom, almost, but not quite, knocking over a lamp on the way.